ROSE'S ALPINE ADVENTURE

Rose is in need of excitement. Taking a leap of faith, she flies to the Alps to take up the position of personal assistant to Olympic ski champion Liam Woods. Though she's never skied before — or even spent much time around snow — that's not going to stop her! But she hadn't bargained on someone trying to sabotage Liam's new venture . . . or on her attraction to him. Can she and Liam save his business — and will he fall for her too?

SPECIAL MESSAGE TO READERS
THE ULVERSCROFT FOUNDATION
(registered UK charity number 264873)
was established in 1972 to provide funds for research, diagnosis and treatment of eye diseases. Examples of major projects funded by the Ulverscroft Foundation are:-

- The Children's Eye Unit at Moorfelds Eye Hospital, London
- The Ulverscroft Children's Eye Unit at Great Ormond Street Hospital for Sick Children
- Funding research into eye diseases and treatment at the Department of Ophthalmology, University of Leicester
- The Ulverscroft Vision Research Group, Institute of Child Health
- Twin operating theatres at the Western Ophthalmic Hospital, London
- The Chair of Ophthalmology at the Royal Australian College of Ophthalmologists

You can help further the work of the Foundation by making a donation or leaving a legacy. Every contribution is gratefully received. If you would like to help support the Foundation or require further information, please contact:

THE ULVERSCROFT FOUNDATION
The Green, Bradgate Road, Anstey
Leicester LE7 7FU, England
Tel: (0116) 236 4325
website: www.ulverscroft-foundation.org.uk

CHRISTINA GARBUTT

ROSE'S ALPINE ADVENTURE

Complete and Unabridged

LINFORD
Leicester

First published in Great Britain in 2019

First Linford Edition
published 2021

*A catalogue record for this book is available
from the British Library.*

ISBN 978–1–4448–4735–2

Published by
Ulverscroft Limited
Anstey, Leicestershire

Set by Words & Graphics Ltd.
Anstey, Leicestershire
Printed and bound in Great Britain by
TJ Books Ltd., Padstow, Cornwall

This book is printed on acid-free paper

1

Rose's phone rang just as the luggage collection point was announced. 'Hi, Mum,' she said as she trooped over to carousel four with the rest of her fellow travellers. The black belt was slowly churning around but was empty of luggage.

'Hello, darling. I'm ringing to see whether you've arrived safely.'

Rose smiled — although she was twenty-eight this was the first time she'd flown abroad by herself, and only the second time she'd flown anywhere. Her mum was both excited and worried on her behalf.

'The plane ride was fabulous, Mum, not a hint of turbulence. I'm just about to pick up my case.'

'Have you seen him yet?'

Rose laughed. Her mum was as clueless as she was when it came to travelling by plane.

'Not yet. I've still to get out into the main terminal building. He's not allowed into this bit of the airport.'

Rose spotted her holly-green suitcase trundling along on the conveyer. She started forward and followed it as it sedately went its way around the carousel. The crush of people was so thick that she couldn't get close to the belt and watched in dismay as it headed off into the distance.

'I hope he knows what a bargain he's getting with you,' said her mum.

Rose tucked her phone under her ear and tried to battle through the crowds in pursuit of her case. 'You would say that, I'm your daughter. I'm very lucky to be working for him.'

Rose heard her mum grumble in disagreement as she dodged a swinging elbow. The holiday maker mouthed an apology at her and Rose smiled in response. She didn't know why she'd put off leaving home for so long — people were very friendly.

'Are you listening to me, Rose?'

'Sorry, Mum, I'm chasing down my suitcase.'

'Why? Where on earth has it got to? I told you not to buy one with wheels.'

Rose laughed and stopped moving. It was no use. Her suitcase was disappearing back into the bowels of the airport. As other suitcases were doing this and no one was getting alarmed, she decided to get closer to the carousel and hope that it reappeared soon.

'It's fine, Mum. Now what were you saying?'

'I was saying that you mustn't undersell yourself. You're an amazing person and a fabulous worker. You'll do a brilliant job.'

'Thanks, Mum. Look, I've got to go. My suitcase is coming into sight again and I need both hands to grab it.'

'OK, love, it sounds like you're already having an exciting time. Call me when you arrive at your destination.'

'Bye, Mum,' said Rose.

She grinned as she dropped her phone

into her pocket. Goodness knows what picture her mother must have in her head about what she was doing. She probably thought Rose was running around an empty airport chasing a runaway suitcase!

This time around she managed to haul her luggage off the carousel with only a little difficulty. Fortunately everyone was in such a good mood they didn't seem to mind being bumped by her suitcase as she wobbled it out of the crowd and turned it in the direction of the exit.

Her heart started to pound painfully as she entered a corridor and realised there was only a short walk to the main lobby where her new employer would be waiting. She stopped, ran her fingers through her short blonde hair and smoothed out wrinkles on her peacock-blue coat.

Liam Woods had emailed her yesterday and told her he would wait for her under the big clock in the middle of the concourse. She'd be able to see it as soon as she came out of the exit tunnel, he'd told her, and he'd be wearing a black jacket with blue jeans.

He hadn't needed to give her such an exact description; she knew what he looked like. His picture had been splashed all over the papers when he'd won gold at the two last winter Olympics for his slalom races, the only British skier to ever achieve such a feat. The media had loved him and there had been numerous articles when he'd announced his retirement last year.

Since then he dropped off the radar but that didn't mean she'd forgotten his wide smile and dark, glittering eyes.

She stepped out into the concourse and looked around. A crowd of people jostled for position at the edge of a roped cordon but, even without looking at the name cards they held, she could tell that none of them were Liam.

She peered over their shoulders and spotted a square clock dangling from the ceiling a few metres away. She skirted the crowd and stopped.

Her new employer was checking his watch even though he was standing under a giant clock. His physique was wirier than she'd expected from the many photographs she'd seen of him but perhaps that was because he was normally encased in ski wear. His dark hair was cut short and his famous, relaxed smile was worryingly absent. Even from this distance she could see the tension in the tight line of his shoulders.

He looked up from his watch and his eyes swept over the crowd, lingering on her for a second. She managed a weak smile in his direction but his gaze continued on without acknowledging her. His shoulders slumped as he checked his watch again.

She fought her legs as they urged her to run back onto the plane towards the safety of home and made them walk the several shaky steps towards him.

'Hi,' she said when she was only a couple of metres away from him. 'I'm Rose.'

Brown eyes widened as his gaze quickly swept from the top of her head to the soles of her feet. He blinked slowly and Rose shifted on her feet. He suddenly remembered his manners and held out a large hand for her to shake.

'Hi, I'm Liam.' His palm was warm and dry and she wished she'd thought to wipe hers on her trouser leg first. She probably felt horribly clammy after a few hours on the flight.

'Is that all your luggage?' he asked, peering behind her.

'Yes.'

'It's not much.'

'You said the room was small so . . .'

'Yes, I did, you're right.' He pushed his hair back from his forehead making it stand up in short, dark spikes. 'Shall we head to my car?'

He went to grab her case but she was still holding onto it. It made for an awkward tussle. Rose hid a nervous giggle but kept a tight grip on her bag. She hadn't had anyone help her for a long time and she preferred to keep it that way.

He gave up after a moment and she followed him as he cut a path through the crowds waiting for tour operators to direct them.

Liam still hadn't spoken to her by the time they stepped into a dark, echoey car park, which unfortunately reminded her strongly of a murder scene in many of the intense dramas she liked to watch on TV. As they reached his dark blue 4x4 she was seriously regretting not running back to the plane when she'd had the chance.

He popped open the boot, and this time she allowed him to pick up her suitcase and stow it inside. She walked round to the passenger door and pulled it open, but before she could climb inside he joined her. For the first time she saw a hint of his famous smile lurking in the shadows of his eyes.

'This is the driver's side,' he said. 'The driver sits on the opposite side in Italy,' he explained.

'Oh.' She looked inside the car and sure enough the steering wheel was on the left, just where she had been about to climb in. Heat flooded her face. She'd known Italians drove on the other side of the road. She'd just forgotten, but now she'd made herself look foolish and untravelled. Not a good start with her new employer. She shuffled round to the other side of the car and climbed in.

The car smelled of sweet cleaning products and the dashboard had a light sheen across its surface. It was a thousand times neater than the car she shared with her mum at home. She folded her hands on her lap and silently reassured herself for the twentieth time that she'd made the right decision and it was all going to be OK.

'Thanks for coming out at such short notice,' Liam said as he reversed out of the space.

Rose studied him covertly as he navigated the narrow lanes of the car park. Up close she could see dark shadows underneath his brown eyes. They almost blended in with his tanned skin but now she realised he had the look of someone who hadn't had a good sleep in a while. Liam glanced at her quickly before negotiating a tight corner and she felt heat creep up her neck at being caught staring.

'Bushells said you were their best all-round temp,' he commented.

'Well they would say that, wouldn't they? They wanted you to hire me,' she joked. From the look on his face this wasn't what he wanted to hear. 'But I am very good,' she added lamely.

She turned away from him as the car pulled out of the car park and into the early evening darkness. She was making a real hash of this! She'd seen the pictures of his face in the papers and she'd imagined he'd be a fun and relaxing boss — not this taciturn man who seemed desperately on edge. When she'd daydreamed about her new job she'd pictured them sharing quirky banter almost immediately, and this hideously stilted conversation was the exact opposite of that scenario. She had to hope he was as nervous as she was and that his smiles would appear when they got to know each other better.

'Perhaps you could tell me a bit more

about the job and the sort of thing you'll want me to be doing?' she said tentatively.

'Did Bushells not tell you?'

'They told me I'd be doing a bit of everything. I'd like to know a bit more detail about what exactly 'everything' entails.'

He scratched his chin, looking a little bemused.

'They told you the basics though, didn't they?'

He was frowning as he concentrated on the road. 'You know I'm running a high-end ski chalet?'

'Yes,' she said. She waited as he pulled out onto a motorway. Car lights twinkled red as far as the eye could see. She peered into the darkness trying to make out details in the landscape. 'Where's the snow?' she asked eventually.

'It's too early in the season for it to snow at this altitude. There's snow in the mountains, though, so don't worry. Do you ski or snowboard?'

'Um ... ' She felt sure her answer

was going to disappoint him but he might as well know the truth because if 'everything' included giving skiing lessons, he was going to be bitterly disappointed. 'I don't do either.'

The tyres hissed through a stretch of water.

'Right . . . ' He didn't look disappointed but it was hard to read his expression when she'd only known him a few minutes. He cleared his throat.

'So, the job is a genuine Girl Friday one. I need someone to help me with every aspect of running the place — laundry, cleaning, cooking and admin. This is my first season, so the job is going to be fluid as I work out what needs to be done.'

'Sounds straightforward,' she said, relieved he hadn't expected her to ski as part of the job.

'There'll also be plenty of time off each day so you can learn to ski.' He glanced across at her again. 'I'm assuming that's why you're out here.'

'Oh yes,' said Rose, nodding vigorously

despite the fact that she had no intention of ever putting on a pair of ski boots!

She'd wanted adventure, and to do something new and out of her comfort zone. She'd applied for lots of jobs abroad and Liam had been the first person to accept her.

However adventure was one thing, hurtling down a mountain on equipment that didn't have brakes was quite another!

'I'd offer to teach you myself but I'll be busy with the guests. I can point you in the direction of the good ski schools.'

'Fabulous,' said Rose.

If he was going to be busy then he need never know that the only thing she was going to be doing with snow was making snowmen.

Having grown up near the coast she'd only ever experienced a light dusting of snow, never enough to even make a decent snowball. She was determined to make up for it now. Then, when the season was over and she'd gained some experience, she would head off somewhere warm and sunny to work. The world was her new playground and she was going to enjoy herself.

He indicated and pulled off the motorway. Ahead, mountains stretched into the distance and Rose could make out the beginnings of snow.

'The forecasts are for a good winter,' said Liam. 'I'm sure this season will be a great success.'

His words were so positive, so why did she have the suspicion he thought the exact opposite?

2

Liam rested his hands on the kitchen work surface and took a deep breath. He'd be all right. This season wasn't going to be a disaster.

Rose was going to be fine. OK, so she couldn't ski or snowboard, she couldn't speak Italian and she looked like a mild breeze would knock her to the floor, but she was cute with big blue eyes, a blonde pixie-cut, and an easy smile. She'd be a hit with the customers ... providing she was as good as Bushells said.

In his jeans pocket his phone vibrated. He dug it out; there was only one person it could be.

'Hi, Mum,' he said as he wandered over to the large stainless steel fridge. He might as well have a drink. He didn't need to be anywhere until mid-afternoon tomorrow and he desperately wanted to unwind. His normal relaxation techniques didn't seem to be working — but then he'd never sunk all his money into one venture before.

'Hello, darling. Did your new Girl Friday turn up?'

'Yeah,' he said, cracking open a bottle of lager.

'What's she like?'

'Short and thin.' He didn't mention her large blue eyes and pale skin. If his mother got even the slightest hint that he found his new assistant even vaguely attractive she'd be booking a church!

'I wasn't asking for a physical description, darling. I want to know if she's going to be any good at her job. Your dad and I don't want you to be let down again.'

Liam smiled. His mother was interested in what Rose looked like. She was an eternal optimist for grandchildren and was always looking to match him with someone. For the last ten years he'd been busy training as a slalom skier and hadn't had the time for a serious relationship, and that hadn't bothered his mother, Doreen. Now he'd given all that up it was a totally different story.

'Rose came highly recommended,' he said.

His stomach tightened as her comment about Bushells wanting him to employ her crossed his mind. He'd been let down so many times in the last few months that he couldn't take it if it happened again.

'Hmm,' said Doreen, unconvinced. Perhaps because of his lacklustre response.

'Mum, I only just met her. She seems friendly and smart but time will tell.'

'All right, love. What time do your guests arrive?'

'I've got to get to the airport for two tomorrow. Anyway, I'd best go. I said I'd give Rose a tour after she's had time to freshen up.'

'OK, darling. Good luck for tomorrow.'

'Thanks, Mum. Bye.'

He put the phone down, more relaxed than he had been for the last couple of weeks — although that could be because he'd nearly finished his bottle of beer, rather than because of his chat with his mother.

There was still no sign of Rose so he went through to the staff sitting room and settled in one of the two armchairs. The room wasn't big but he'd told the decorators he wanted it to be cosy and they'd done a good job. Two deep-cushioned chairs flanked a wood burner, which he would put on later, and a thick rug lay on the floor between them. There was a TV but as Rose didn't speak Italian and he didn't watch much, it was unlikely to be used. Besides, the chairs were pointing away from it so it was hardly the focal point.

'This is snug,' said Rose, entering the room.

'It's for staff only,' said Liam, standing up to greet her.

'It's a great room for relaxing at the end of the day,' she said softly as she spun on the spot and took in the whole space.

She was trying to be so positive but

he could see the doubt lurking at the back of her eyes. He'd become good at reading people. It came in handy when assessing the confidence — or lack of — in his competitors.

The only thing he wasn't sure of was the source of her unease. Could it be him? He hadn't been at his friendliest. He was trying, but he was so convinced she was going to let him down that he was wary of relaxing his guard. He was so far removed from his normal behaviour even he didn't recognise himself. It was the first time in years he'd done anything without his teammates. It was terrifying going it alone.

Or could it be that she was nervous? She was in a foreign place, about to do something out of her comfort zone. He should forget about his own hang-ups and concentrate on putting her at ease.

'Would you like a glass of wine or a beer?'

'White wine would be lovely, thank you.'

'Excellent. If we head back to the

kitchen I'll get you a glass and then take you on a tour of the rest of the chalet.'

He pulled open the fridge and got out a bottle of wine and another beer. He'd stop after this one. He wasn't a big drinker but the last few months had been tough and the first drink had definitely eased the knot in his stomach.

'My first guests are arriving tomorrow at two,' he said as he glugged the wine into a glass. 'I'll leave here around one to get to the airport in time. There's not a lot left to do this time. Because I didn't know if I'd get anyone to come over in time and help, I've done everything myself. You can have the morning off to explore if you like. The town is only ten minutes walk away, or you can take the car if you don't fancy the trek back uphill. I'll give you those instructor details, but if you could be back before one that would be great.'

He handed her the full glass and returned the bottle to the fridge.

'I'd like to be able to offer them hot drinks when they arrive — they're all kept in the cupboard up there. And some canapés. If they don't want to go skiing tomorrow afternoon then there's alcoholic drinks cooling in here,' he opened a small fridge, which was set into the cupboards. It was stacked full of every drink he could think of.

'We'll need to keep this stocked at all times. A lot of the reason people come on skiing trips is to eat and drink a lot, and the holiday experience is all-inclusive. You did say you cook, didn't you?'

'Yes, I can cook. I'm quite good at it even if I do say so myself,' she smiled shyly.

'Do you have any catering qualifications?'

She paused, 'No, but I have worked in lots of kitchens and I've been the main cook in my household for many years.'

He ran his fingers through his hair. Dare he ask what sort of thing she could cook? He hoped her experience wasn't in some sort of burger joint and that home-cooking meant more than just opening a can of beans. With the lack of time to find a replacement after his first Girl Friday had pulled out, he hadn't been able to be choosy.

He knew his way around the kitchen and could put together something if he had to, and he had an arrangement with a restaurant in town to supply meals if it did go pear-shaped. He mustn't panic. The squirming in his stomach didn't calm down even as he reassured himself.

He took another swig of beer and then headed through to the main house, his new assistant padding after him.

'Wow,' she said as she stepped into the living area.

He smiled, momentarily forgetting his anxiety. Her reaction was exactly what he'd hoped for when he'd had this room designed.

'This is stunning,' she said.

She made her way over to the wall of glass that took up the length of the living room. It looked out onto the mountains and although there wasn't much to see in the darkness of the evening, you could make out clusters of twinkling lights where villages nestled into the side of steep slopes. It was a view that never failed to transfix him and which he'd made the most of wherever he could throughout the chalet.

'The dining room is through here.' He turned and pointed to the left.

A large oak table took centre stage in the room and the same floor-to-ceiling windows took up the whole of one side.

'It's exquisite, Liam,' she said, running her hands over the tabletop.

A tingling sensation zipped down his spine at the sound of her saying his name. How odd! He'd not felt anything like that before. The long days of working flat-out must be getting to him.

'Upstairs are the bedrooms. I'll leave you to take a look at those by yourself. For now we'll head downstairs.'

He took her down a level, all the while aware that he wasn't being very friendly. He wanted to say or do something to put her at ease but his own tension was getting to him, preventing anything coming to mind. The more he thought about it, the worse it was getting until his tongue felt tied into a tight knot.

He hadn't slept properly for weeks. Despite sinking all his money into this venture, problems kept springing up like a leaky pipe. He'd raced around trying to patch everything up but the sensation of everything being held together by budget sticky tape was difficult to shift.

The latest disaster had been the assistant he'd met and interviewed, who cancelled at the last minute. She'd been perfect, with exemplary references and with such a passion for being on the slopes that she'd worked in ski resorts for the last ten seasons. When she'd phoned to say she couldn't come because she'd broken her ankle only a week before she'd been due to fly out, he'd been dismayed.

Rose had come to his rescue but he was so worried she was going to be the cause of the next disaster to befall him that he couldn't appreciate her arrival properly, even though it meant he was no longer alone.

'The games room is through here.'

He gestured through an open doorway towards a pool table. 'I think the guests will spend a lot of time in here so it needs to be kept clean and tidy. But ... this is my favourite room.'

He stepped aside so Rose entered before him.

'Oh wow, I wasn't expecting anything like this,' she said, her voice filled with gratifying awe.

Liam stepped into the room after her and watched her reaction play across her face as she took everything in. If his guests were only half as impressed as she clearly was, then he was on to a winner. This room had taken almost all his savings but hopefully it was worth it and would push his accommodation above his competitors'.

The low-level lighting made the water of the pool glisten invitingly. He wondered if Rose would like a dip but quickly shook his head. Thinking of how good his new assistant would look in a swimming costume was not the way to go.

'These glass doors slide open,' he said,

briskly moving over to show her. 'And out here is a hot tub. You still get the view down here but hopefully it's more sheltered from the slopes than the living area upstairs.'

She came and stood next to him outside, her breath instantly making puffs of icy air.

'This house is like something out of a fairy tale,' she said.

'I'm glad you like it,' he said, pleased.

Something inside him finally relaxed, and this time it wasn't just because of the beer he'd drunk. Only his close family had seen the results of months of hard work. They'd all told him how much they liked the chalet but they were family and were always on his side, even when he made terrible decisions. It meant a lot to him that someone who didn't have to be nice thought his holiday home was as special as he'd planned.

'Who cleans the hot tub?' she asked.

He laughed, 'Not you or me. I've got a specialist cleaner to come out every week and inspect it.'

'Phew! I didn't fancy spending my time scrubbing it while a snow storm rages.'

'You won't volunteer to scrape the driveway when it's covered in snow then?' he teased.

'No way!'

Liam hid his grin behind his beer bottle as she seemed to realise she'd been quite forceful in her reply and perhaps that wasn't the best way to talk to her new boss.

'I mean,' she clarified. 'I don't think I'd be very good at that. I'm not particularly strong.'

Liam found himself nodding. She did look as if a reasonably sized snowball would knock her to the ground.

'You're not supposed to agree with me,' she said with mock indignation.

He laughed, surprising himself with how carefree he sounded.

'We don't need to worry about clearing the snow either. A local firm comes and deals with it.'

'Phew,' she said, stepping back into the

warmth. 'Is there anything else to see?'

'Downstairs is a locker room. It'll get a bit grubby with snow and mud being dragged in but we'll both clean that when we get a free minute.'

She nodded and he realised that her wine glass was empty. He was about to offer a top-up when she spoke.

'Great — well, if that's all, I think I'd like an early night. I'm exhausted from all that travelling.'

Liam resisted the urge to check his watch. It couldn't be late, maybe eight-thirty. She hadn't travelled that far and she didn't look tired. If anything she looked wired, but her body was turned away from him and she was giving off signals that she'd like to get away. Not the most auspicious of starts but he hadn't been his most welcoming. Hopefully tomorrow would be better.

3

Fat flakes of snow were swirling in the air as Rose stepped out of the chalet early the next morning. How her younger brothers would love all this snow! She snapped a quick photo on her phone and sent it to them via WhatsApp.

Then she crunched her way down the driveway and headed towards the small town which Liam told her had the nearest shops. He'd offered her the use of the car, saying she was insured to drive it, but the idea of getting behind the wheel when lots of the roads were covered in snow did not appeal.

Although Liam had given her the morning off, a quick glance at the fridge told her he'd not prepared any food for the guests arriving that afternoon. She'd quickly looked up Italian meals on the internet but decided against following any of the recipes on her very first day.

Instead she'd written down the ingredients for her favourite lasagne dish and decided to go with that.

Her handbag also contained the handwritten details of the local ski school. Liam presented her with it when she set out. She'd smiled and thanked him politely and then shoved the paper into her bag where it would remain for all time!

The centre of town wasn't big; it was more of a large village. She found the supermarket and inside it was frantic with people calling to one another in all kinds of different languages. Vegetables were heaped in overflowing boxes. Rose found an abandoned basket and began to fill it with peppers, tomatoes and aubergines.

Before long her basket became too heavy to carry so she pushed it along with her foot to the back of the long, winding queue at the cash desk.

'Excuse me,' said a voice from behind her. Rose turned to find a tall, thin woman of around her own age smiling shyly at her. 'I think you were on the plane with me yesterday. I'm Hannah.'

'I'm Rose,' she said, taking Hannah's hand. 'I did fly out here yesterday. I'm working as a chalet girl for the season.'

'Me too!' squealed Hannah. 'I was hoping to find someone else doing the same job. Perhaps we can meet up and compare notes sometime.'

'I'd love that,' said Rosie, pushing her basket forward as the queue moved.

'Here,' said Hannah, scribbling something on a piece of scrap paper, 'Take my number and text me when you've got a free hour or so. Hopefully we'll be able to organise something, although if this is anything like my last season there won't be a great deal of time to meet up.'

'Is it very busy then? This is my first season.'

'Oh, yes. It's incredibly busy but crazily good fun. You're going to love it.'

Rose smiled as she hefted her basket onto the conveyer belt. 'I really hope so. I've not done anything like this before.'

'I'd never snowboarded before last

year either but you'll get caught by the bug really quickly and you'll be desperate to come back next year.'

Rose smiled politely as the contents of her basket were whizzed across the till and almost thrown at her on the other side. She wasn't about to confess that she had no intention of going out on the slopes. Would everyone think she was a bit weird if she didn't?

Why else would she work during the winter in a ski resort? If she said it was her first taste of adventure would she sound horribly naïve? Perhaps she'd have to give skiing a go, even if she did stick to the flattest of slopes. At least then she'd have something to tell people.

She stuffed as much of her shopping as she could manage into her rucksack and filled up another two carrier bags with produce.

Liam's credit card paid for everything. She wasn't sure if she should wait for Hannah or not but as her shopping was being flung past the till at the same alarming rate she thought it wouldn't be long before Hannah was ready to go too.

The carrier bags cut into Rose's fingers as the two girls made their way back up the slope. The snow had stopped, leaving a bright blue sky in its wake. The glare from the sun reflected on the snow lining the roads and Rose realised why so many people wore sunglasses. It clearly wasn't a fashion statement after all. She made a mental note to buy herself a pair next time she came down to the town. Who'd have thought you needed sunglasses around all this snow?

'Do you think you'll learn to ski or snowboard?' asked Hannah as they rounded the first bend.

'Um, I'm not sure yet.'

'I took up snowboarding last year but I'd like to try a bit of skiing this time around. I'm hoping to get a glimpse of Liam Woods. You know, the gold winning slalom skier? He bought a chalet here and it's opening this season. It's the biggest news in town.'

'Yes, I do know. I'm working for him.'

Hannah stopped in her tracks.

'No way! How did that happen? I think every chalet girl or boy I've spoken to applied to work for him and no one even heard back.'

Rose frowned — that didn't seem likely. From what she'd gathered from Liam he'd been almost desperate for staff. Maybe Hannah was exaggerating. She glanced at her new friend. Hannah was still gawping, waiting for her response.

'I got the job through an agency. I only met him very briefly. He seems OK.'

'OK? The man's a living legend! Not to mention the fact that he's drop-dead gorgeous. You are the luckiest girl I know.'

'Well...' said Rose, thinking of the dark shadows under Liam's eyes and the tense set of his shoulders, 'I'm not sure he appeals to me but I can try and get you an introduction when I know him a bit better.'

'That would be amazing, thank you. But I don't want to put you in an awkward position with your boss so don't worry if you can't make it happen. I'd like the two of us to meet up anyway.'

'Me too,' said Rose, smiling at Hannah.

They turned another corner and the ski slopes came into view with white-topped mountains stretching for miles ahead of them.

'Isn't it just stunning?' said Hannah.

'Yes,' said Rose, her breath catching in her throat, 'It really is.'

Back at the chalet Rose chopped and fried onions, peppers and courgettes and soon she had two thick sauces bubbling away in large pots on the hob. While she waited for them to be done she fished the oven manual out of a drawer and flicked to its index. She'd just found the right section when her phone rang. Balancing it in one hand and the instructions in the other she answered. 'Hi, Mum.'

Rose had already called her mother last night and texted her this morning but she should have known that wouldn't be enough. They'd so rarely been apart for all of Rose's life that this must be just as strange for her as it was for Rose.

'Is everything all right, darling? Did

you find everything you needed at the supermarket?'

'Yes, I'm just working out how to use the oven but other than that everything is under control.'

She still hadn't mentioned to her mum how unnerving she'd found Liam. When he'd been relaxing last night, she'd seen glimpses of the man she'd been expecting but most of the time he'd been serious and on edge. Not the sort of boss she'd hoped to have.

'Are you making your delicious lasagne?'

Rose glanced at the instruction booklet again and pressed a button. The oven hummed into life.

'I am and I've found some lovely-looking crusty bread to go with it. You should see the fruit and veg out here, Mum. They're twice the size of the stuff we have back home. I'm going to put together a salad to go with it.

'That sounds fabulous, darling.'

Rose smiled as she pressed another button and promptly frowned as the oven completely shut down. She'd obviously misunderstood the instructions, she glanced back down at them.

'Thanks, Mum. How are the boys?' she asked because her mum would expect her to.

She half listened to her mum's answer on how her younger brothers were doing. She repeatedly prodded the first button she'd tried and which had originally been so productive but nothing happened. Had she already killed the oven?

'When do your guests arrive?' her mum asked.

'In a couple of hours. Look, I've got to go … '

'OK, darling, Dan and James send their love.'

Rose made an inarticulate noise, which she hoped sounded like, 'Lovely, please send mine back,' and not, 'Aargh! I think I've destroyed the oven on my first attempt!'

Barely aware of her mum saying her goodbyes Rose opened the instruction booklet at the beginning. She was still poring over it ten slightly sweaty minutes later when Liam walked in.

'Hey,' he said softly, seemingly very subdued. 'Everything straightforward in there?' He nodded to the instruction booklet she was clutching.

'Oh yes, very,' she said, unable to admit things weren't going quite as well as she'd hoped.

'Great.' He fiddled with the strap of an empty plastic bag. 'I've had a phone call from the party coming today and their plane's been delayed by four hours.'

'Oh,' she said, dropping the instruction book and looking up at him.

The black shadows under his eyes were even deeper today than they had been last night and his shoulders were drooping slightly. She wasn't sure if that was an improvement or just as bad.

'Will you go and wait?' she asked.

'No, I'll head out and check a couple of the runs I'll take them on tomorrow. Hopefully there's been enough snow to make them viable.'

Rose nodded as if she had a clue what

this meant. There was snow everywhere so of course there would be some on the runs.

'This is the business phone for the chalet,' he continued, holding out a smartphone. 'I won't have any signal on the slopes so it's best if you keep hold of it in case they ring with an update.'

'OK,' she said, taking the phone from him and placing it on the worktop. 'When will you be back?'

'I'll be back by four and I'll head straight to the airport. Something smells good,' he indicated the dishes behind her. 'What are you making?'

'I've put together four lasagnes. One meat and one veggie for tonight, and two more for the freezer. I'm just trying to work this oven. Any suggestions?'

'Sorry, I've not used it before. If that's all I'd best be off ... '

He was half-turned to the door already. Guessing that skiing kept him calm, she just smiled and gave him a brief wave goodbye. She kept the smile on her face until she heard his feet on the stairs pounding down to the locker room.

By her reckoning she had five hours to get this oven working. Hopefully it wouldn't take that long.

When she'd finally deciphered the instructions she wrote them out in her own words so that she'd never have to read through the booklet again. Its maddening linguistic errors had nearly had her tearing her hair out. She followed her own writing and successfully got the machine working.

Satisfied, she flicked on the kettle. She'd reward herself with a cup of tea and a chocolate biscuit before she started putting together the dessert. Thank goodness she'd decided to work out how to use the oven hours in advance. If she'd had to deal with that level of stress with guests around and Liam getting tenser and tenser, she didn't think she'd have been able to do it.

The phone rang just as she was settling into one of the comfy armchairs in the staff lounge. She pulled hers out expecting it to be her mother but the screen was oddly blank. It took her a second to realise that the noise was coming from chalet's phone.

'Hello, Liam Woods' chalet, how may I help?' she answered in her most professional voice.

'Hello, this is Bryn Davies. We've arrived at the airport and there's nobody here to collect us.'

Rose gasped and glanced at the clock. It was two in the afternoon, the exact time the Davies party was due to arrive at the airport, so why had Liam gone off skiing?

'I'm so sorry,' she said quickly. 'We were told the plane had been delayed but we've obviously been misinformed. I'll be with you as soon as I can. In the meantime, please take a seat at the cafe and we'll reimburse any costs you incur.'

'All right then. We'll see you soon,' said Bryn.

Rose crossed her fingers that she'd made the right call. Hopefully nothing in the cafe would be that expensive and Liam's profit for the week wouldn't be destroyed before he began.

There was no point ringing Liam but she tried his number anyway. She left a message explaining the situation, hoping that she sounded calm and collected. Then, just in case he didn't listen to his messages she wrote him a note and pinned it to the fridge with a magnet.

She remembered to climb into the car on the left-hand side and then she had a thought. Running back into the chalet she grabbed two bottles of prosecco froom the fridge and plastic glasses and dropped them into her rucksack.

Back in the car, she turned the key in the ignition and the sat nav flickered into life. She hardly ever drove at home and she had never driven abroad. Her fingers shook slightly as she clicked onto the sat nav's menu. A wave of relief rushed through her as the local airport came up as the last destination. She pressed the button to show her the route and gulped as she realised how winding the first part of the journey was.

She took a deep breath and started

the engine. She'd wanted adventure and to do something different … and now was the time to start.

4

Liam slung his skis over his shoulder and began the short trek from the edge of the slopes to the chalet. The runs were almost perfect; a few spots here and there could do with more snow but nothing to worry about. A heavy downfall was forecast towards the end of the week so his guests would have nothing to complain about on that front either. The perfect weather was one less thing for him to worry about.

He glanced out towards the driveway as he made his way down to the locker room but it wasn't until he was storing his skis that he realised what he'd seen or, more accurately, what he'd not seen. His mind must be playing tricks on him because that couldn't be right.

He sprinted back up the stairs and stood on the driveway staring at the place his car had been when he'd left earlier. It wasn't there. He glanced at his watch. It was time he left to get to the airport so where on earth had Rose taken the car?

Perhaps she had forgotten something from town and had just nipped out quickly. He jogged to the end of his driveway to see if she was heading this way, but the streets were quiet and there were no cars heading towards the chalet.

He patted his pocket and then remembered he'd switched his phone off and left it by his bed. There was no point taking it out onto the slopes as he never had any signal out there. Besides, he didn't want to get distracted. For him, skiing was always about being in the moment.

Heart pounding, he raced back into the chalet. Taking the stairs two at a time he nearly stumbled as he careened into the staff kitchen. As he righted himself he noticed a note pinned to the fridge. His blood ran cold as he read through it.

Bryn Davies and his party couldn't have arrived at the airport on time. Bryn had phoned him this morning to let him know about the delay. Rose must have become confused — but at least she was at the airport. If he could make sure she waited for the party, then all was not lost.

He went through to his room and turned on his phone. A message popped up from Rose and he listened to it as he pulled off his salopettes and hunted around for some jeans. Her voicemail was calm and concise. She'd received a phone call from Bryn saying that he'd arrived and she'd gone to collect him. She'd left two hours ago. She sounded so sure that he began to doubt himself.

Heading back into the kitchen, he fired up his laptop and searched for the airport's website. Sure enough Bryn's flight was listed as on time.

He sank down onto a kitchen chair as heat rushed over him. He couldn't understand why he hadn't gone online to check earlier. It was easy enough to do. But then he had no reason to suspect the phone call from Bryn wasn't the real deal. He dropped his head into his hands and groaned. His first paying customers had arrived and he'd stood them up. This was not a good start to the week.

It was as if this whole venture had been cursed from the very beginning. It had taken far longer than it should have just to buy the plot of land where the chalet now stood. Documents had gone missing and the project had stalled for a couple of months. He should have taken that as a sign, and gone into his family business like his parents had suggested. If he'd coupled his earnings with them with the savings he'd made he'd probably have been able to retire early and travel the world. Now he'd wasted his money on this project, which seemed doomed to failure.

The press would have a field day if he got bad reviews. As his younger brother had jokingly pointed out the press had raised him so high after his Olympic wins that the only way was down.

He debated ringing Rose to see where she was but decided against it. If she was driving up the mountainside she wouldn't thank him for phoning and distracting her. He'd driven that route hundreds of times and the sharp turns and steep drops never failed to make him slightly queasy — even though he was used to heights and travelling all over mountainous regions.

He stood abruptly. It was no use sitting here worrying about things he couldn't change. He needed to do something.

Stacked neatly on the kitchen counter were ingredients for some sort of cake — at least that's what he assumed the eggs, flour and sugar were for. A worn cookbook was open, face-down next to it. He picked it up and found it open to a chocolate brownie recipe.

He pulled out a large mixing bowl and began to measure out the ingredients. It was surprisingly therapeutic melting chocolate and butter over a large saucepan of boiling water. He stirred the mixture and found that if he focused on it intently he could almost forget about his abandoned passengers and his nearly empty bank balance.

By the time he'd poured the batter into a baking tray he'd convinced himself that he wouldn't mind working with his parents after all. They all got on well and although he didn't have any interest in cars he supposed he could —

He was pulled out of his daydream by the sound of the front door opening. He held his breath and then … laughter and chat filled the air.

He let his breath out slowly. That didn't sound like people who were monumentally annoyed.

He pasted on a smile, the smile he normally reserved for the press when he wanted to convince them he was fine about losing a race when he really wasn't, and made his way into the main living area.

'Liam,' cried Rose, as soon as she spotted him, 'Here are your guests.' Her eyes were wide and over-bright but she was in one piece and so was everyone else. 'This is Bryn,' she said, pointing to the larger of the two men, 'and this is his wife, Ann, and their friends, Will and Sally.'

Rose came to stand next to him. 'You have chocolate on your chin,' she murmured, quickly reaching up and wiping it off with her fingers.

Her hand was cold where it brushed against him and his skin tingled from her touch long after she'd moved away.

'Your Girl Friday drives amazingly well,' said Bryn. 'We hardly spilled a drop of our drinks on the way up all those hairpin bends.'

'I took a complementary bottle of prosecco with me,' Rose explained, not quite meeting his eye. 'To make up for them not being picked up on time.'

Ah, so that accounted for the good moods. They were all slightly tipsy! Technically all the drinks were free because they'd been included in the price but if his guests thought they were getting a good deal, then who was he to argue?

'I'll go and fetch the luggage,' said Rose.

'No way,' cried Bryn. 'You sit down and relax after that drive.'

In the end it was agreed that all the men would fetch in the luggage and Rose would make some warm drinks for everyone.

Liam was desperate to get Rose alone so that he could talk to her about the airport mix-up, but his guests weren't in a rush to let him go anywhere. Instead they wanted to talk to him about his competition days and because they were paying him a lot of money, he couldn't deny them what they wanted. Together they whiled away a long, lazy afternoon drinking mugs of rich hot chocolate and snacking on a light Victoria sponge that Rose seemed to pull out of thin air.

It was lucky the guests were easy to get along with, because they insisted he join them for dinner. They wanted Rose to join them too, but she said she would rather keep on top of things in the kitchen and excused herself politely.

'Do you have any idea who could have phoned and told us your flight was delayed?' asked Liam as they tucked into Rose's delicious lasagne.

'No idea at all,' said Bryn. 'Perhaps it was someone playing a prank on you.'

Liam nodded as he took a mouthful

of rich tomato sauce. He couldn't for the life of him think of anyone who would think what happened was funny. It had to be someone Bryn knew, because the alternative didn't bear thinking about.

Finally, after what felt like an eternity, his guests retired to their rooms to unpack. Liam cleared up the remaining dishes and took them through to the kitchen where he found Rose washing up. He picked up a tea towel and joined her at the sink.

'Thank you for today,' he said. 'Without you it would have been a complete disaster.'

She laughed brightly and a frisson of pleasure zipped down his spine at the sound.

'It was a pleasure — but can we agree that you do the airport runs from now on?'

He smiled. 'Was it terrible?'

'I have never been so terrified in my entire life! I truly believed the car was going to careen off the side of the mountain on some of those turns!' She waved her arm about to demonstrate how twisty the roads were.

His heart clenched. She'd been frightened and yet she'd done it for his guests — and for him. He wasn't paying her enough. He made a decision.

'On Wednesday afternoon, the guests have to entertain themselves. I'll take you out on the slopes and teach you how to ski.'

'Oh,' she said, dipping a casserole dish into the soapy water. 'Please don't feel you have to. I don't want to put you out.'

'I want to,' he said firmly. 'I'm afraid I can't pay you any more than I already am but if I teach you, you won't have to pay for lessons so that will be a saving.'

'OK,' she said, scrubbing the dish hard.

She didn't sound very enthusiastic but perhaps she didn't realise how much he normally charged for a lesson. He wasn't about to tell her because that make him sound like a bit of an idiot, but maybe he'd somehow slip it into a conversation later, then she might appreciate his gesture.

Next to him her stomach growled, and the tips of her ears turned pink as she tried to smother the sound with her hand.

'Have you eaten?' he asked. She shook her head. 'Leave the dishes and sit down then,' he said, kicking out a chair at the small kitchen table. 'I'll get you something.'

She sat down obediently as he opened the fridge door. There was nothing much inside.

'Is there any lasagne left?' he asked.

'No — it's all gone.'

'All of it? I'm not surprised, it was delicious, but I can't believe five of us got through two whole lasagnes. I'll make you a sandwich if that's OK? Is there anything you don't eat?'

'Great, thank you, and I eat everything except liquorice,' she replied with a smile.

He managed to rustle up a chicken sandwich and a large square of chocolate brownie.

'Liam,' she said — and he felt the same, strange tingly sensation he'd had whenever she'd spoken his name. He cleared his throat, 'Yes.'

'Don't you think it's odd that someone rang you to say the flight had been delayed?'

'Very,' he agreed as he set the sandwich in front of her. She didn't ask but he also poured her a large glass of white wine. She deserved it after her drive earlier.

'And there was something else today ...'

'Oh?' He sat opposite her, though he wasn't sure he wanted to hear what she had to say.

Rose tucked a strand of hair behind her ear where it instantly popped straight back out again. 'I met a girl at the supermarket and she told me that loads of people had applied to be your chalet girl or boy but I got the impression from you that you weren't inundated with people to choose from, hence picking me.' She gestured to herself.

'I am very glad you are here,' he said firmly. 'But you're right. I hardly had any applicants and the ones I did were slightly crazy. One, for example, said that although we'd never met she'd seen a picture of me in a newspaper and she thought we'd have beautiful babies!'

He grinned and Rose snorted with laughter.

'What about the girl who let you down at the last minute? How did she apply?'

'She was recommended by a skiing friend of mine.' He rubbed his chin. 'You know, I've had a lot of setbacks with this project.'

'In what way?' she finished her sandwich and pulled the brownie towards her.

'Do you want ice cream with that?' he asked.

She took a bite and closed her eyes. 'Mmm,' she murmured. 'This is good.'

He shouldn't be staring at his employee's mouth like this. He tore his gaze away and studied the fridge door instead.

'It doesn't need ice cream,' she said as she took another bite. 'Tell me about the other problems you've had.'

'It's nothing major, in fact it's probably

a coincidence but a few things haven't gone as smoothly as they should. I was meant to open last season but everything was so delayed I had to put it off until this year, so I'm a lot more strapped for cash than I'd planned at this stage.'

'Is that why you're so tense?' she asked.

He glanced across at her. A faint blush spread across her cheeks but he didn't mind the personal question. She was right; he was very tense.

He ran his fingers through his hair. He was used to wearing it long and it still surprised him how short it now was.

'Yeah, I'm tense. I need this chalet to be a success or I'm absolutely sunk.'

She nodded, taking this news calmly. He wasn't sure if he should be telling her all this. They'd only just met and she was in his employ but he was tired of struggling on his own and pretending to his friends and family that everything was going swimmingly. Skiing had been so easy. Yes, he'd had to work hard, but it had been straightforward. This enterprise was a whole different ball game.

'Can you think of anyone who might want you to fail?' Rose asked quietly.

'No. In all honesty I can't.'

'People who've lost races to you?' she asked as she scraped the bowl for crumbs.

'No. We all travel round the circuit and meet the same people all the time. We've all lost or won at some point. For the most part we're friends. I can't see why any one of them would want me to fail at this. They'll all be too busy concentrating on the season ahead to think about me anyway.'

'Perhaps it's just a series of unfortunate coincidences then,' she suggested although her expression said she didn't believe that.

He was starting not to believe it either, though he'd meant what he'd said. There wasn't anyone he could think of that would mean him any harm.

'That brownie was amazing, thank you, Liam.'

'I just followed the instructions in your recipe book,' he said. 'Thanks for arranging it all. Do you have a menu planned for tomorrow?'

'I was thinking of some sort of stew with lots of veg and roast potatoes, followed by a crumble. I know it's not even slightly Italian but I know how to cook it.'

'It sounds fantastic to me. No, don't clear up. I'll do it. You have the rest of the evening off.'

'Are you sure?'

'Positive.'

She smiled gratefully at him and made her way to her room, sliding her phone out of her back pocket as she did so. She was on the phone a lot and he wondered briefly if she had a boyfriend back home, before reminding himself that it was none of his business.

5

Rose peered hopefully out of her bedroom window and was met with unending cobalt-blue skies. She sighed and flopped back onto her bed. For the last two Wednesdays the snow had been coming down so heavily, skiing had been impossible. She'd pretended to be really disappointed and then she'd made a run for it, meeting up with Hannah and staying out until she was sure the conditions weren't going to improve in time for Liam to take her out on the slopes. She'd hoped he'd be so busy he'd eventually forget his promise to teach her, but he hadn't.

He'd been so pleased with the way she was working that he'd reiterated the desire to teach her several times. Rose knew he was offering her a huge favour. She'd researched the costs of a private lesson and a standard one was outside her pay cheque — so goodness knows how much it must cost to be taught by Liam!

The thing was that in the two weeks of being here, she still hadn't been hit with the burning desire to get out on the slopes. It wasn't helped by the guests coming back at the end of the day and reliving their spectacular falls in painstaking detail. Bryn, in particular, seemed to spend a lot of time going down slopes on his back.

Besides, it wasn't as if she wasn't doing other adventurous things. She and Hannah had enrolled on a crash course in speaking Italian. They were both equally awful, but it made them and the rest of the class laugh so she didn't mind.

She took another look at the view outside.

There was still no sign of snowfall. In fact it looked like it was going to be a spectacular day. She threw on some clothes and headed out to the kitchen. A young, newlywed couple were this week's guests and they'd been an absolute dream so far. They were so wrapped up in each other that they didn't need a lot of entertaining and, because there were only two of them, they didn't make a lot of mess. She was going to miss them next week when a large party was due.

She pulled open the fridge and took out all the ingredients for a full English breakfast.

'Hey,' said Liam, stepping into the kitchen, still wearing pyjama trousers and an old T-shirt.

She tried not to look as he stretched and revealed a small slice of tanned stomach, but she couldn't quite manage to turn her head away.

'Hi,' she said, taking a gulp of coffee and scalding her tongue.

'Are we on for later?' he asked, opening the fridge door and pouring a glass of orange juice.

'Um, well, are you sure I've got all the right equipment and stuff?'

He grinned, 'Are you nervous?'

'Not at all.'

For some reason she was reluctant to tell him she was terrified of the idea, which was silly. If she said she didn't want to go, he wouldn't make her. He wasn't a horrible boss, in fact he barely acted like a boss at all. He took a good share of the chores even though he spent hours on the slopes teaching his clients.

As nearly twenty days had passed without any further mishaps he'd started to relax. His smiles came easier and the tension in his shoulders had all but disappeared. She liked this version of him far better than the terse man she'd first met.

A few times she'd lain awake worrying she was starting to like him too much. She didn't want to develop a crush on her boss. In a few months, the season would be over and she'd move on. She'd prefer to do so with her heart intact.

'Great, but even if you were nervous there's no need. The slope I'll take you on is like this.' He held up an arm almost horizontal with the floor.

'What was the one like that Bryn kept

going down head first?'

'It was more like this.' He held his arm up at nearly right angles to the floor. She gulped and he laughed. 'You'll be going down runs like that by the end of the season with no problem.'

'I don't think so,' she muttered under her breath as he headed back to his room.

She opened a packet of bacon and placed all the slices on the griddle. She was going to enjoy this breakfast, because tomorrow she might have a broken leg!

She took two breakfasts through to the newly.weds who were sitting at the large dining table sweetly gazing at each other. They barely looked at Rose as they distractedly thanked her for the food. Rose shook her head as she walked away; she couldn't imagine ever being that much into another human being.

Back in the kitchen she plated up breakfasts for herself and Liam. Normally they grabbed cereal or fruit between tasks, but this morning she felt the need for a fortifying meal.

'This looks good,' said Liam, sliding

into a kitchen chair opposite her.

'Mmm,' she agreed around a mouth of bacon.

'I'll be back at one and I'll grab a quick sandwich. Then we can head out.'

Rose concentrated on cutting a sausage on her plate. 'I'm defrosting a lasagne and there's chocolate-orange mousse for dessert.'

Liam flung back his head and laughed. 'Are you telling me this because you don't think you'll make it back later?'

Rose felt heat flood her face and she dipped her head lower to concentrate on her food.

'Hey,' said Liam, reaching over the table and lightly touching her sleeve. 'We don't have to do this if you don't want to — but if we do, I promise I'll look after you.'

She looked up from her breakfast. She could feel his light touch through the fabric of her shirt. His eyes were kind and smiling. She took a deep breath. 'I'd like to try it, but I am very nervous.'

He gave her arm a gentle squeeze. 'I

won't make you do anything you're not comfortable with, and I'm confident you'll enjoy it.'

'What is it that you love about skiing so much?'

'There are so many things I love about it but I suppose it's the sense of peace I get when it's just me and the mountain.'

Rose had been so sure he was going to say he loved the speed or the exhilaration of the race.

'I —' she began.

'Excuse me,' said a voice from the doorway. 'Just to let you know we're ready when you are.'

'Great,' said Liam, downing the rest of his orange juice. 'I'm ready now.'

He stood and strode over to the kitchen door.

'See you later,' he said to Rose and then he was gone.

* * *

The morning passed in a blur of indecision. One minute she was going to tell Liam she just couldn't face hurtling down a slope on something little more sophisticated than a tea-tray, and the next she was excited. By the time Liam came home she was exhausted and he didn't give her a minute to change her mind.

'Go get changed,' he said, as he stood in the kitchen chomping down the sandwich she'd made him. 'I'll be finished in a sec and we'll go out.'

She'd laid her ski gear out on the bed. None of the clothes looked flattering. She pulled on leggings and a long-sleeved t-shirt and then stepped into the salopettes. They were as bulky as she feared. Once she'd added the padded jacket she looked like a brightly coloured snowman.

'Is all ski-wear this ungainly?' she asked Liam.

His eyes crinkled with amusement, 'I think that jacket's too big for you — but you'll be grateful for the extra padding.'

'I thought you said I wouldn't come to any harm,' she protested.

'I meant because of the temperature,' he said, clearly battling a smile.

'Hmm,' she grumbled.

'Let's get going before you start to boil in that.'

She waddled down to the locker room after him. Perhaps she should have gone out and bought her own clothes rather than relying on him to pick stuff out for her. Something more slimline would be better — but ski clothes were another expense she couldn't afford.

'Shall I carry those?' she said, pointing to the extra pair of skis he had over his shoulder.

'No, it's fine. Don't forget your gloves.'

The gloves made her fingers appear to be the size of sausages but as they stepped outside, she was grateful for their toasty warmth. Although the sun was high in the sky the air was freezing. She followed him around the side of the chalet and along a well-worn path, her ski boots making an unusual crunching sound as she moved.

In front of her Liam dropped both sets

of skis to the ground.

'Getting into skis is quite simple,' said Liam as she caught up to him. 'All you need to do is —'

'Hang on, I'm not putting the skis on here!' Rose didn't care if she sounded rude to her boss. He'd clearly gone mad. They were standing at the edge of a very steep slope.

'We need to ski to the beginner's slope,' Liam explained patiently.

'I can't ski,' she said slowly and clearly. Liam seemed to have forgotten that salient fact!

'I know. I'm going to guide you down.'

'Can't we walk?'

'No. Now fit your foot in here.' He took her left leg and slotted her boot into a ski. Before she could protest, he did the same to her right leg.

'Wha-ah,' she wailed as she slowly began to move without any conscious effort.

'Where are you going?' he asked, grabbing hold of her arm. 'Wait for me.'

'I'm not doing anything — the skis

just started moving by themselves!'

She heard his snort of laughter in response but she was too terrified to look at him. The only thing stopping her from hurtling down the mountain was his strong grip on her arm.

'Right,' he said when his own skis were on.

He stood behind her and placed his skis either side of hers. Then he slipped his right arm around her and pulled her back against his chest so that their skis were parallel and their bodies were touching. The gesture would have been shockingly intimate if they hadn't been separated by several layers of thick clothing.

'Try and relax,' he murmured into her ear, his breath brushing her skin, as they slowly began to make their way to the slope.

'I've changed my mind. I'd like to go home now,' said Rose as the dangerous-looking precipice got ever closer.

All she heard was the low timbre of his chuckle as he edged them out onto the slope ahead.

Rose's heart thundered loudly in her ears.

'Relax and let me guide you,' he murmurmed.

Rose swallowed a scream as she glanced down at the slope which dropped away in a steep incline. People covered it everywhere, careening down at impossibly high speeds.

'I'm going to take us down now. Trust me.'

'I do trust you,' she said. 'It's me I don't trust. I'm incredibly clumsy. I should have told you that.'

In answer he pushed them forward and this time Rose did scream. She felt Liam laugh against her back and then they were flying. The wind rushed against her face as they traversed across the mountainside. Her heart-racing terror slowly faded under Liam's controlled guidance.

'How was that?' asked Liam as the ground flattened beneath them.

'That was ... that was ... actually, it was fun!' she said, her knees shaking and her heart pounding frantically.

Liam laughed and slowly moved his skis away from hers until he was standing next to her. She missed his reassuring presence.

'Let's hit the beginners' slope and see if we can get you moving by yourself.'

Liam showed her how to move over the ground with skis on. The motion was a little like roller skating only with huge planks of plastic strapped to her feet instead of wheels.

'There are only children on this slope,' commented Rose as they approached a small hill covered in young people careening confidently in every direction. She hadn't a hope of being as good as them...and they were mostly twenty years younger than her.

'I can take you elsewhere but this is the flattest slope around,' said Liam, stopping to look at her and grinning when he caught the look on her face.

'It's OK, the fewer adults the better. That way there'll be not so many people around to witness my humiliating attempts to stay upright.'

'I think you're going to surprise yourself.'

'I think you're the one who's going to be surprised,' she said. 'I'm willing to bet you've never seen anyone as inept at this.'

He laughed and bent over to move her skis into an inverted V position.

'This is called a snowplough ... ' he began.

* * *

Hours later Rose lay on her back and contemplated the sky. The blueness had a different quality to it over here than it did in Britain. Perhaps it was because they were so high up or maybe it was something to do with all the bright, white snow. Whatever the reason, it was breathtakingly beautiful. She wished she had her camera so she could capture the vividness but she'd left anything breakable back at the chalet — which had been a good move, as she'd have squashed everything by now. 'Are you going to get up?' asked Liam, his voice laced with laughter.

'I'm enjoying lying down down here.'

'Sure it's not 'cos you're too lazy to stand?'

'I think you've forgotten what hard work it is to get upright when you've got these strapped to your feet.' She waggled her skis to demonstrate.

He laughed and flopped down onto the ground next to her. 'I fall over all the time.'

She turned towards him and raised an eyebrow. He grinned. 'Well, perhaps not all the time but enough to remember how to get up again. How about this for a deal — you get up and we ski down to the town and I'll buy you a hot chocolate. We can get the bus back up to the chalet.'

'I'll do almost anything for a hot chocolate,' she said. 'OK, then if you help me up I'll try not to knock anyone over on the way to the town.'

He chuckled and, with an ease Rose

couldn't emulate, pushed himself to standing. Reaching down a hand, he pulled her up too. She wobbled precariously but managed to remain upright.

'Right, I'll race you to the bottom. Get set, go!' he said, his eyes full of mischief.

'Ha, very funny,' she said, smiling back at him.

Out on the slopes he was a different person from the one she saw in the chalet. Even when he was relaxed there he was never as smiley, nor was his laughter so close to the surface. She could see that he was born to be out here.

Slowly she began her descent. Her leg muscles were screaming at her to stop and let them rest.

'Don't forget to bend your knees,' he shouted.

'If I bend them any further I'm going to be doubled-over,' she called back to him.

She heard the faint rumble of his laughter and she grinned to herself. Making him laugh had been the unexpected highlight of her day and they had laughed an awful lot. Every time she'd fallen over or skied in the wrong direction they'd been unable to stop themselves collapsing into hysterical giggles. She still couldn't see the attraction of skiing, but she could at least understand the fun of trying to learn. Maybe lessons wouldn't be so bad after all, so long as they were all with Liam.

Outside the cafe Liam showed her how to unclip her skis from her boots then he stuck them in a purpose-built rack next to hundreds of others.

'Did you enjoy this afternoon?' he asked as he pushed open the cafe's front door.

'Yes, I did actually,' she said, following him into the welcome warmth.

'You sound surprised.'

'I thought it would be painful,' she confessed.

'It can hurt when you fall but you were going slowly and these slopes are padded with deep snow.'

'I was going very fast!' she protested. The ground had seemed to whizz past her feet whenever she'd stayed up for more than a minute.

'Yes, you're the Usain Bolt of the slopes,' he grinned and winked at her. 'Do you want marshmallows and cream with your drink?'

'Yes, please,' she said. 'I'll grab us a seat.'

She found two chairs near the wood burner and settled herself comfortably into the chair. This was an aspect of skiing she could get into!

She unclipped her boots and slipped her feet out of the uncomfortable bindings. She held her stockinged feet to the warmth of the fire as Liam returned with the hot chocolates.

'Thank you,' she said as she took hers from him. Her fingers brushed his as she did and her hand tingled at the contact. 'And thank you for today. I wasn't sure I would enjoy my lesson but I had a lot of fun.' She scooped up a spoonful of cream and popped it into her mouth.

'Great,' said Liam, who seemed to be watching her eat, 'I enjoyed — '

'Liam,' interrupted a soft, breathy voice.

Rose glanced up at the woman standing over them. She may as well have been part of the furniture as the stranger only had eyes for Liam.

'Sarah,' said Liam, jumping up from his chair and enveloping the newcomer in a hug. 'What are you doing here?'

Rose took a mouthful of cream as she watched Liam disengage from Sarah. Sarah, she noticed, did not look like a giant snowman in her skiing outfit. Instead Sarah's clothes fitted snugly around a tall, slender figure, while long, blonde hair fell artfully around her face. Rose didn't like the stab of jealousy that hit her out of nowhere.

'I know what I said over the summer but I was missing the season so I came out,' said Sarah, her light grey eyes never leaving Liam's face.

'Oh, right . . . well, it's lovely to see you. Are you staying for long?' asked Liam.

'I've managed to get a teaching gig for a couple of weeks so I'll be here until the end of December at the earliest although I'm hoping to extend it to the end of the season. Perhaps we could go out for a drink to catch up?'

'That would be… yeah, I'd like that,' said Liam and Rose took a large gulp of her hot chocolate.

She'd known developing a crush on her boss was a bad idea and this afternoon's skiing lesson had made things a lot worse. Now she'd spent time with him she'd seen just how gorgeous he was when he was relaxed and enjoying himself.

It was painful to realise that she was out of his league. She couldn't even begin to compete with the lady who now held his complete attention. Still, it was better to find out now than fall for him and have her heart crushed at a later date.

'I'll call you,' said Sarah, giving Liam a long, lingering gaze before she strode away.

Liam slowly sank back into his seat. He was so absorbed in his own thoughts he appeared to have forgotten Rose was sitting next to him. She studied him as she sipped her drink, the rich chocolate comforting on her tongue.

'Are you OK?' she asked softly when it was clear he wasn't going to speak any time soon. She'd nearly finished hers while the whipped cream on his was melting over the edge of his mug.

He jumped at the sound of her voice. 'Sorry, I was a million miles away.'

He picked up a spoon and quickly demolished his cream. When he began gulping down the chocolate she thought he wasn't going to answer her question, so she was surprised when he said, 'I'm fine. I was surprised to see Sarah, that's all. We dated for a while. It was the longest relationship I've been in but when push came to shove she wanted to settle in Britain, while I wanted to come out here for at least half the year. A normal nine-to-five job would kill me. Anyway, we couldn't reach a compromise so we split up.'

Another unpleasant stab of jealousy hit Rose but she firmly squashed the sensation down. She would be his friend and his employee and hope for nothing more. To do otherwise would be unbelievably foolish, especially now the beautiful Sarah was out here, meaning the reason for their split was gone.

Liam took another long mouthful.

'She was quite adamant that it was time to settle down and do something sensible with our lives so the fact that she's out here is strange, especially when I'd heard she was enjoying life in Wimbledon.' Liam shook his head, 'Sorry you don't need to know all this ancient history.' He raked his hands through his hair and it stood up in now familiar spikes. Rose resisted the urge to reach up and stroke it flat. 'You did well today. If you get a chance to practise before next Wednesday remember to bend your knees.' He glanced at his watch. 'Are you all right to catch the bus by yourself? I'd like to get a few runs in before it gets dark.'

'Yes, I can manage from here. It's only walking to the bus stop.'

Before she'd finished speaking he'd

downed the rest of his drink and stood up.

'Great,' he said. 'I'll see you later.'

He strode briskly out of the cafe, leaving Rose sure of two things: despite his protests he was bothered by the arrival of his ex-girlfriend … and even though she didn't want to be, Rose was jealous.

6

Rose checked the oven timer. In two minutes the carrot cake would be ready. The creamy topping was already on the counter waiting to be added once the cake was cool.

'Hello,' called a voice from just outside the kitchen. 'May I come in?' Mrs Murphy, the leader of this week's group of eight guests, poked her head around the door. 'Of course,' said Rose, who liked this rowdy extended family.

'Is there any food for the boys? Only they're hungry yet again. I think the delicious smells coming from this kitchen have set them off.'

'There are sandwiches in the fridge and washed fruit in that bowl.' Rose indicated the glass dish on the kitchen table. 'I've got sponge cake in the tin as well. The cake you can smell will be ready when you all get back from skiing this afternoon.'

'You're an absolute legend,' said Mrs Murphy, opening the fridge. 'Are you sure I can't tempt you to come and live with me full-time?'

Rose laughed and opened the oven door, letting the pleasant warmth wash over her. Inside, the cake was a delicate golden brown. She set it down on the counter and lightly touched the top. It sprang back promptly when she took her fingers away. Perfect.

'Are you skiing this afternoon?' Rose asked as she used her spatula to slide the cake away from the edge of the tin.

'I'd like to relax in the hot tub but I suppose I should join them,' Mrs Murphy pulled a face but Rose wasn't fooled, the woman loved her family.

'There's always time for the hot tub later.'

'That's true but it will be filled with boys then.' Mrs Murphy shuddered in mock horror and Rose laughed. Out of all their guests so far the Murphy clan were the most enamoured with the hot tub, spending lots of time in it when they weren't skiing or eating.

Rose upturned the cake onto a cooling rack, 'I'll cut you up some sponge and bring it through to you,' she said.

'Thank you,' said Mrs Murphy, her arms full of sandwiches. 'I'll take these out to everyone.'

Rose smiled at Mrs Murphy's retreating back. Feeding this family was a full-time job but they were so loveably boisterous and free with their enthusiastic compliments that working for them wasn't a chore. She opened a cake tin which held the Victoria sponge she'd made yesterday. She cut a large chunk off and then sliced the rest into slightly smaller pieces.

'Hey,' said Liam, emerging from his bedroom and joining her in the kitchen. 'I hope some of that is for me.'

'I cut you this piece,' she said, handing him the plate with the large chunk on it.

'The Murphys aren't going to eat the rest of it, are they?' he asked, picking up his plate and taking a large bite.

'I think they probably will but don't worry. I've just finished mixing up another one and it will be going in the oven soon.'

'You're an absolute godsend,' he mumbled around a mouthful of cake.

'Mrs Murphy pretty much just said the same thing. She asked me to go and live with them full-time,' Rose laughed.

'I hope you told them you weren't going to.'

Her heart skipped a beat at the sound of panic in his voice. She knew his concern was only because he'd come to rely on her cooking and not because he particularly wanted her, but even so, she liked that he needed her. No matter how many times she'd told herself not to develop a crush on him her body was intent on betraying her.

'I'm not going anywhere,' she reassured him.

She was gratified to see the look of relief flash across his face.

'Great,' he said. 'Right, I'll take this through to the Murphys so they don't make any further bids to poach you. I'll also hurry them along. The Snake's Head pass should be quiet at this time of day.'

He left with a brief smile and her heart lurched. She rubbed her eyes; maybe she should have a holiday fling with one of the other chalet workers. That might distract her from her boss and these unwanted feelings. As far as she knew, he hadn't met up with Sarah yet. It would almost be better for her if he did. Although it would hurt if they rekindled their romance at least her heart might get the message that he was out of bounds.

She shrugged and concentrated on pouring the Victoria sponge batter into a clean cake tin. After a while she heard the distinct sound of the group clomping down to the locker room. The house descended into blissful silence as Rose gently smoothed the frosting onto the top of the carrot cake. When she'd sprinkled some crushed walnuts over the icing, she surveyed the kitchen. Every counter and table top was piled high with unwashed dishes and leftovers from lunch. She'd need to clear everything away before she started on the next epic meal she had to prepare if she was to keep the Murphys satisfied.

She quickly stacked all she could into the dishwasher but she was still left with a mountain of pots and pans. She flicked the tap on and turned to the table to collect the first pile.

It took her a few seconds to grasp something was wrong.

Turning back to the sink she realised that instead of filling the washing-up bowl the water was slowing to a trickle. She turned the tap to full but the water continued to slow. She snapped the tap off and then tried again. The water trickled slowly out and then came to a complete stop.

'OK,' she muttered, 'This is probably a temporary problem. The water's been switched off for a moment. I'll go and tidy the games room and then try again. It's nothing to worry about.'

She switched the tap off in case the

water came back on in her absence and flooded the kitchen and then she patted it encouragingly. Hopefully this was only a passing blip.

A whirlwind had obviously hit the games room since she'd last left it. Board games were scattered across the floor, pieces from different sets intermingling with abandon. Not a single pool cue was in the rack and there wasn't a dart anywhere near the dart board. For an hour she lost herself in sorting out the chaos. Her younger brothers would find this sort of work desperately dull but she found returning items to their correct place rather soothing. When all the cues were back in the rack and the games were neatly stacked on a shelf, she went back to the kitchen.

She flicked the tap on again but apart from a rumbling pipe deep in the chalet's hidden mechanisms nothing happened.

A dread curled in her stomach. If she couldn't get these pans clean, she couldn't make dinner and this lot of guests were constantly hungry!

She came to a stop, her hands resting on the kitchen worktops as she stared out of the kitchen window. Never mind the washing up. What about the rest of the house?

The chalet depended on running water. The guests would want showers or baths when they came back from their afternoon skiing session. And there was the hot tub they all loved so much. What about heating? Did that depend on water?

She touched the radiator. It was cool but that didn't mean anything. The house was so well-insulated she rarely had the heating on when she was alone in the day.

After finding that the first shower didn't work she didn't really need to test the rest but she did anyway, hoping that water would miraculously gush out of one. When she was satisfied the water had well and truly stopped she rang Hannah.

'Hello,' answered Hannah, 'I'm glad you called. Are we still on for our Italian lesson tonight? I'm in the mood for a laugh.'

'I'm not sure,' said Rose slowly. 'I think I might be in the middle of a crisis. Has your chalet got running water?'

'Yeah, of course. Why?'

'The water's completely stopped here, and I've got a ton of washing up.'

'OK, don't panic. I'm on my way.'

'You don't need —' But Hannah had already put the phone down.

* * *

'Us chalet workers stick together,' said Hannah when she arrived ten minutes later carrying a large plastic box.

'Thank you so much for coming over,' said Rose, her knees weak with relief at the sight of a friendly face.

'Let's go through to the kitchen and we'll stack the dishes into this box. I'll take it all back with me and wash them all for you.'

'You don't need to do that!' Rose exclaimed.

'Don't be daft. I know you'd do the

same for me. Wow!' Hannah stopped in her tracks. 'Would you look at this place? It's like a palace compared to my workplace.'

Hannah slowly turned in the centre in the living room, her jaw gaping as she took in the floor to ceiling windows, 'It's stunning,' she breathed. 'No wonder the locals are worried.'

'What do you mean?' asked Rose, plumping up discarded cushions and putting them back on the sofa.

'Oh, nothing,' said Hannah, turning away from the window and facing Rose.

'What's nothing?' asked Rose, a niggle of worry bubbling up in her stomach, made worse when Hannah's face flooded with colour.

'Ignore me. I shouldn't mention nasty gossip. I'll only stir up trouble where there's none.'

'You're going to have to tell me now. Nothing can be as bad as I'm imagining,' cried Rose.

'Oh, really, don't! It's only a couple of the other chalet owners moaning, and saying they can't compete against an Olympic medallist and his swanky apartment. But that's bonkers, isn't it? There's something out here for everyone's budget. No one who could afford to stay here would come to the chalet I work at, for example.'

'How bad is the hostility towards Liam?' asked Rose, pulling on the end of her sleeve.

Hannah cringed. 'I really wish I hadn't said anything at all. You're looking very anxious and it really is nothing. It's just a few grumpy owners with sour grapes because they were never good enough skiers to win Olympic medals. Almost everyone else is excited to have him out here and I think his presence will bring more people to the area. Now let's get your washing-up sorted.'

Rose led Hannah into the kitchen but she couldn't concentrate on her friend's bubbly chatter. For the first time she had tangible evidence of people against Liam. It might explain the malicious phone call and the problems he'd had before the chalet had opened. But the thing that worried her most was today's water disaster. Was it a coincidence or was it an escalation of the problem? Was it her overactive imagination conjuring up a problem when there wasn't one?

She forced herself to concentrate on what Hannah was saying. 'I'm sorry, what did you just say?' she asked.

'I said that I rang a few friends on my way over here and no one else seems to be experiencing any problems with their water.'

Rose smoothed her jumper flat against her stomach. She wished Hannah hadn't mentioned the lack of water to a lot of people. She didn't want word getting round the small town that Liam was experiencing problems. It was probably too late now — the cat was already out of the bag.

'Right,' she said, shaking her head and concentrating on the main problem. 'I was thinking I should check the water supply to the house but I've no idea where to go for that.'

'Shall we try the locker room? Is that

downstairs? The water might be coming into the house there.'

'Thanks, Hannah but you've already helped me so much. I'll have a hunt for the pipework myself and let you get back to your own job. I know how pressured it is trying to get everything done while the guests are out of the house, and doing my dishes is going to make your day even more stressful.

'While I think of it, do you have details of the local takeaways? I'll need to give the guests dinner without creating any more washing-up.'

Rose kept up a steady chatter of meaningless conversation as she walked Hannah back to the front door. Although she liked and trusted her new friend, Liam deserved to know of her suspicions first. If this water shortage turned out to be an attack on him, then she was sure he wouldn't want his problems to be common knowledge.

'I might not make the Italian class tonight. It depends on how easily fixable this water problem is,' Rose said as she helped Hannah load the dishes into her car.

'OK — call me and let me know. Are you sure you don't want help finding the water pipes?'

'No, it's fine, thanks. You've been amazing.'

Rose smiled and waved as Hannah drove slowly down the driveway, the wheels of her car crunching over the crushed snow. When she could no longer see the car she let herself back inside. The house felt considerably cooler than normal so obviously the lack of water was affecting the heating.

She fingered her phone deep in her jeans pocket. The urge to phone her mum for help was almost overwhelming but there was nothing her mum could do except worry, so Rose left it where it was. If the water was coming into the house at the lowest level, it would make sense for the pipework to come in at some point in the locker room.

She headed down the steep steps to her least favourite room in the chalet.

Despite all her efforts it always seemed to smell of unwashed socks and no matter how many times she vacuumed, mud seemed to coat the floor. As the door was often open to the outside, there was no central heating installed and standing around in it without a coat was making her fingers freeze.

She rubbed her arms through her thick jumper as she stood at the edge of the room. Most of the lockers were standing open, with trainers or shoes shoved inside and not much else. A discarded glove lay on the floor and she picked it up absently and laid it on the bench in the middle of the room. Liam's locker was locked shut, as was her own, but she couldn't imagine there was any pipework in either of them.

She did a complete circuit, looking around the floor space for anything that might vaguely resemble a water pipe. When nothing obvious jumped out at her, she sat on the bench in the middle of the room and looked up at the ceiling.

She snorted; what was she doing? As if

the water would come in above everyone's heads. It had to come in underground, but where? She tapped her fingers against her wooden seat. If she didn't come up with the answer soon she was going to have to go and get a coat.

Maybe she was wrong. The chalet was built on the side of a mountain, so technically almost all the floors could be considered as being on the ground floor. She couldn't take another minute in this icicle-cold room.

She stood and as she did so the top of the wooden bench wobbled slightly. Bending down she grasped the edge of it and pulled.

Sure enough, the wooden top came off in her hand. Underneath, boxed in on every side, were pipes leading to a stopcock. The problem was immediately obvious. Where the lever for the stopcock should have been, all that remained was a stump. She bent down to take a closer look.

Using the tips of her fingers she tried to push the lever into the opposite position, but there wasn't enough left to get a good purchase.

She ran her fingers over the end of the stump. If Liam had accidentally snapped the handle off he would have told her, or it would be lying around somewhere.

There was only one obvious conclusion: someone had deliberately tampered with it.

7

Liam laughed at something one of the Murphy boys said as he pushed his skis back into his locker. The whole family were in high spirits after today's run on the slopes.

Liam's own good mood was for a completely different reason. One he didn't want to dwell on too much. Tomorrow was Wednesday, which meant he had the afternoon off — and it also meant he would be spending it uninterrupted with Rose as he took her on another skiing lesson.

He followed the noisy family back up to the main living area.

'Oh,' he said stepping into the lounge and spying Rose hovering oddly in the middle of the room. 'Are you going somewhere?'

Rose was wrapped up in a coat with her bobble hat firmly wedged onto her head.

On the table behind her were steaming mugs of hot chocolate and plates of carrot cake.

'No, I'm not going out,' she said, with a voice he recognised as forced jollity. 'But there's been a bit of a change of plan for this evening's entertainment.'

She smiled at the Murphys who all smiled back at her. The younger members decided they couldn't wait for her to explain and set upon the table of snacks as if they'd never eaten before.

'I'm afraid,' Rose said, 'that we're having a bit of trouble with our water so I've taken the liberty of booking you a meal out at the Antica Pizzeria. It's got a fabulous reputation and, because the baths aren't working, I've also arranged for you to go to the leisure centre in the centre of town.

It's an open-door heated pool, a bit like our hot tub but on a much larger scale. I thought the boys would love it because it has some cool slides.'

'It's all complementary, of course,' said Liam in a voice he didn't recognise as his own.

Rose nodded, smiling mechanically. Something was very wrong. Liam's heart started to pound.

'That sounds great!' said Mrs Murphy, oblivious to the tense undertones. 'But are you sure? We don't mind a bit of cold while you sort the problem out.'

Liam glanced at Rose who gave a slight shake of the head. 'That's very kind of you,' he said. 'But I don't want to put you out.'

'I've already booked a taxi,' said Rose. 'It'll be here in about forty minutes.'

She was obviously keen to get the guests out of the house. Whatever had happened to the water was far more serious than Rose was letting on.

'We'd best get changed then,' said Mrs Murphy, hurrying the boys upstairs and grabbing her own hot chocolate and cake on her way past the table.

'What's happened?' asked Liam when his guests were out of earshot.

'Someone has switched the water off and then broken the lever on the stopcock so it can't be put back on,' said Rose in a rush of words. 'I'm sorry to be so blunt but there's no other way to say it. I'm sorry.'

Liam turned and ran back down to the locker room, Rose following close behind. He pulled the seat off the wooden bench revealing the pipe work underneath.

'Do you see what I mean?' Rose asked quietly.

Liam nodded slowly, unable to take his eyes off the broken lever. He leaned in to get a closer look at the pipework — perhaps the lever had been accidentally snapped off and the remains were underneath everything. When he couldn't see anything, he ran his fingers underneath but found only dust.

Rose stood behind him, waiting patiently.

'The broken lever isn't here,' he said. 'Did you take it out when you found it had been broken?' he asked desperately.

'No, I couldn't find it either.'

Liam stood slowly and gently put the

seat back on, covering up the pipework.

'It's been broken deliberately and someone's taken the lever with them so we can't fix it,' he said, an odd calm setting over him.

'It looks that way. Do you think one of the Murphy boys broke it by accident then hid the broken bit because they worried we'd be angry?'

He turned and looked at Rose. She clutched the knot of her scarf and tugged it away from her throat as if it were choking her.

He shook his head, 'I don't think so. They've only been in here when I have too. Plus, they seem like well-behaved boys. I don't think they would have it in them to do something like this and then act as if nothing had happened.' He paused and looked back at the damage. 'Then again, why would someone do such a thing? I don't think I've ever upset anyone enough to make them this angry at me.'

Rose pulled a face. 'Well, I heard some things today ... ' She shifted from one foot to the other and looked down at the floor.

Liam's heart thudded. All this time he'd thought the hurdles he'd faced had been coincidental but to find there was malicious intent behind them made his legs weak.

He sank slowly onto the bench. 'What have you heard?'

'It's probably nothing but . . . ' She paused, unwound her scarf and pulled it off over her head. 'Hannah, she's one of the other chalet girls, you know?' He nodded, he did remember the name. She was a new friend of Rose's that he'd not met yet. 'She said some of the local chalet owners are resentful of you and this chalet.'

'Really? What on earth for?'

She shrugged and a hint of a blush spread across the top of her cheeks. 'Something to do with you being an Olympic medallist and owning a swankier chalet than any of theirs.'

He paused to take that in. 'I don't think that's enough of a motive to try and sabotage me.'

'Perhaps not, but the fact is that someone has done this deliberately.'

He nodded and rubbed his eyes. He was so tired. He wanted a bath and a beer and then to collapse on the sofa to watch something undemanding on the TV.

'Can you replace the stopcock?' Rose asked, breaking into his thoughts.

'I'm going to have to. The guests can't sleep in a freezing cold house. Neither can we, for that matter. Let's go back upstairs and see if I can phone a local plumbing shop.'

Back in the lounge, the Murphys were getting ready to leave in a flurry of bags and bulky coats.

'I'm so sorry about this,' said Rose, taking Mrs Murphy's hand in hers. 'Thank you so much for being so good about it all.'

A wave of gratitude for Rose washed over Liam as he watched her talking to his guests. She was fantastic at putting people at their ease and the Murphys clearly loved her. Thank goodness she was there to smooth things over, because he would be useless without her. All he could think of right now was getting the lever fixed.

He flicked on his phone as Rose helped his guests out to the waiting taxi. His fingers fumbled as he tried to type into the search engine and he realised he was shaking.

He put the phone down and took a deep breath. This problem wasn't insurmountable. When it was over, he would sit down and try and work out who disliked him so much that they would try and sabotage his business. But for now he had to focus on getting the stopcock fixed.

'Did you find anything?' asked Rose as she came back in, bringing a rush of cold air with her.

'Yes, but I have to go to the Turonia industrial estate. It'll take a couple of hours.'

'I'll come with you.'

'Thanks. I think that's probably for

the best. It'll be freezing in here once the sun sets completely. At least you'll be warm in the car.'

She smiled. 'I'm ready to go when you are.'

'I'll go and grab my wallet.'

Liam raced back to his bedroom and picked up his bank cards from beside his bed. Fortunately stopcocks weren't that expensive. He was barely turning a profit so far this season. This would make a small dent in his finances, but a new boiler would have been a lot worse.

* * *

It was midweek so the roads were fairly clear of traffic as he followed the tight corners towards the base of the mountain. Beside him, Rose sat rigidly still with her eyes tightly closed. He grinned in spite of the seriousness of the situation.

'I don't like the edge,' she said, without opening her eyes.

The road did skirt the edge of the

mountain with very little room for error. He was used to travelling roads like this, but he supposed sheer edges could be scary if you weren't.

'How did you manage when you went to pick up Bryn and company?' he asked.

'With great difficulty!' she confessed.

He laughed, 'You were amazingly brave. Or did you drive with your eyes closed?'

She smiled and he noticed a dimple at the corner of her mouth. He dragged his gaze away. He needed to concentrate on the road ahead and not on the way his employee looked. One wrong move and they would be plummeting down the mountainside to certain death.

'I kept my eyes open while driving Bryn and his family, I thought it best I see the road.' She grinned. 'I think my panic about getting the guests from the airport overwhelmed my fear of edges. If you asked me to drive now I don't think I could.'

'I owe you a great deal,' said Liam, wishing he could better express how grateful he was.

'I was just doing my job,' she replied softly.

Liam shook his head. 'No — your job is to cook some food and help me keep the place clean, not fire-fight ridiculous problems.'

Rose shrugged. 'My life was pretty … well, not boring as such, but every day was pretty much the same. I came out here for adventure — and I'm getting it in spades!' Before Liam could ask about her life prior to the chalet she asked, 'Have you given any more thought to who could be behind this?' Her eyes flickered open for a second before she squeezed them shut again.

'No. Did you hear anything when you were alone in the chalet earlier?' he asked her.

'No. I was trying to think when I used the water last. I had a shower this morning and then I washed up after breakfast. I must have used it since then but I can't pinpoint the exact time. The breakage could have happened any time during the morning. I didn't hear anything unusual in all that time. But you can't really hear anything from the locker room in the kitchen.'

'I had a shower before lunch so someone must have snapped it after I'd taken the Murphys out for the afternoon skiing. I didn't notice anything unusual in the locker room before we left.'

'That means someone must have been watching the chalet, because it wasn't long after that you left that I noticed the problem.' She paused. 'That's a bit creepy.'

Liam's hands involuntarily gripped the steering wheel tighter. How dare someone come into his chalet when Rose was there on her own! What if she'd walked in on the person while they were in the process of snapping the lever? Would they have hurt her? It didn't bear thinking about!

'If I could open my eyes for a few minutes I'd write a list of suspects,' said Rose, her light-hearted comment making him chuckle despite the anger coursing through him.

'I don't think we have any suspects, do we?'

'Well, there's the other chalet owners.'

'I don't suppose Hannah gave you any names?' he asked.

'No. She seemed embarrassed to have mentioned anything at all. I could ask her, although I'm not sure what we'd do with the information.'

The ground levelled out and Liam pulled onto the main road to Turonia, the nearest city. 'You can open your eyes now,' he said.

'Oh, wow!' she exclaimed as her eyes flickered open and she took in the view. 'The snow's reached the bottom of the mountains. It looks like something out of a children's picture book.'

Liam smiled at Rose's reaction. He was used to snow, he'd lived and breathed the stuff for so long that it only interested him if there wasn't enough of it to have a decent ski, but Rose's reaction was like a child's. Her face was pressed up against the passenger window and he slowed the car so she could take in the passing scenery.

'It's beautiful,' she sighed.

He kept quiet for the remainder of the journey, allowing her to enjoy her first glimpse of snow-covered Italy without intrusive thoughts of suspects and vandals.

All too soon he pulled into the large industrial estate, which could only be described as functional, and Rose lost interest in the surroundings. He followed the directions on his sat nav, allowing the disembodied voice to guide him through the rabbit warren of nearly identical roads.

'When will you next see Hannah?' he asked. 'Doesn't she take Italian classes with you? You could somehow slip it into the conversation.'

'The next one is Saturday.'

'I thought you had a weekday one, too.'

'Yeah, the class is meeting tonight. I don't think we'll make it back in time.'

'Tonight? Why didn't you say? You

could have kept warm in class instead of coming with me.'

He glanced across at her as he pulled into the plumber's warehouse car park. Under the light of a street lamp he could make out a faint blush in her cheeks. His heart skipped a beat. Could it be that she wanted to be with him as much as he wanted her company?

He couldn't allow himself to think like that. He mustn't try and take advantage of the one person currently saving him from absolute ruin! But if she'd welcome his interest that would be a whole different ball game.

The problem was, he'd never met a girl like Rose before. She was so sweet and caring and she depended on him to make a living. If he got it wrong, he knew she would be embarrassed as much for him as for herself. He held his breath as he waited for what she was would say next.

'I didn't want you to be on your own,' she confessed. 'It can't be a good feeling knowing someone's out to get you.'

So that theory went out the window — she felt sorry for him! He felt his own cheeks heat.

'Well, thanks,' he said gruffly. 'I appreciate it but now I feel terrible that I put you through the ordeal of coming down the mountain when you could have been with your friend.' He pulled into a parking spot, feeling like a prat.

She cleared her throat. 'I do have another idea for a potential suspect.' She stared out of the front window and didn't comment any further.

'Are you going to tell me?'

She nodded slowly. 'I don't think you're going to like it, though.'

He rubbed his forehead, 'Don't worry about me. I have a thick skin. Tell me.'

'I was thinking — and I have no evidence so I could be wrong — but you were telling me about how much she wanted you to move to Britain and so I thought this would be an idea . . . I mean, it would be good for her if you failed and everything.'

'Who are you talking about?'

She took a deep breath and turned to look at him. 'Your ex-girlfriend, Sarah.'

8

The chalet was still and quiet. Rose sat at the kitchen table and drummed her fingers on the surface. For the first time in nearly five weeks she wanted to go home to her mum. She longed to breathe in her mum's comforting floral scent and to relax into a warm and loving hug. With Christmas coming, she was missing her family.

Although Liam had taken her suggestion that his ex-girlfriend might be behind the malicious incidents at the chalet well at the time, he'd become increasingly distant. Now, nearly a week later, she wished she'd kept her thoughts to herself. She'd obviously offended him deeply and their easy camaraderie had vanished.

Decision made, she phoned home.

'Hello, darling,' came her mum's warm voice. Although not as good as a hug, the muscles in Rose's neck did relax, leaving her floppy with tiredness. 'Hi, Mum,' she said, trying to inject her voice with enthusiasm. It didn't work.

'What's wrong?'

'Nothing, how are the boys?'

'The boys are fine. Now tell me what's wrong.' Rose sighed quietly. 'Please tell me, Rose. Have there been any more nasty incidents?'

'Why do you think something's wrong?' asked Rose. 'Couldn't I have just phoned for a chat?'

'You forget that I know you better than anyone, darling. I can tell from your voice that something has upset you.'

'I'm not upset. I just felt a wave of homesickness and I wanted to hear your voice.'

'Oh, love,' said her mum softly. 'We miss you too, but you sound like you're having quite the adventure so do stick it out.'

'I'm going to. I miss you all so much though.'

'Of course you do. We're all so amazing, you were bound to miss us!' her mum joked. 'So, are you going to answer my question? Have there been any more nasty incidents?'

'No, nothing in over a week. Perhaps whoever it was has given up. Changing the subject, do you have the recipe for that hummingbird cake? I want to give it a go. Our guests this week have a birthday coming up and I thought its exotic ingredients would be a bit special.'

Rose wrote the recipe down as her mum read it out, her familiar voice soothing Rose's worries.

'Do you think you'll be able to get all those ingredients?' her mum asked.

'I should think so, Mum. I'm not completely in the middle of nowhere. They do have shops here.' Rose grinned.

'I can't imagine a town half-way up a mountain. You must send me more photographs.'

'I will, Mum. Now I'd best get on. I have to make a coq au vin and I want to give it enough time to let the chicken slow-cook in the sauce all afternoon.'

'I hope you're not working too hard.'

'No, of course not, Mum. But I do need to feed the guests.'

She didn't add that she had been working extra hard this week, anything to distract herself from the fact that Liam was distant and preoccupied.

She took her time slicing mushrooms and onions. Her unprecedented level of hard work meant that only the meal was left on her to-do list today. She'd rung Hannah earlier to see if she was free this afternoon but her friend was busy.

Perhaps, if Rose was brave, she'd take the bus down to the beginners' slopes and have a little practice. After three intensive lessons with Liam, she was reasonably confident that no serious harm would come to her. She wasn't quite confident enough for a proper run but brave enough to try it with lots of people around to help her up if she landed in an ungainly heap.

She was sliding the casserole into the oven to slow cook when the chalet's phone rang.

'Hello, Liam Wood's chalet, how may

I help you?' she said as she answered it.

'My name is Colin Fairweather,' came an officious voice. 'I'm booked for next week. In light of the reviews I'm cancelling. I've sent an email but as no one bothered to respond, I'm calling.'

Rose couldn't think of a single thing to say. She'd checked the business email account only a few hours ago and there had been nothing about cancellations in the inbox.

At the other end of the phone Colin Fairweather let out a long sigh. 'I can see I'm dealing with incompetents here. Let me put this in a way you can understand. Return my deposit and I won't get my lawyer involved.'

Colin Fairweather put the phone down. Knees shaking, Rose went through to the staff sitting room and switched on the laptop they used for the chalet business. Colin Fairweather's email was as brutal as his phone call.

To whom it may concern,

I'm writing to cancel my booking for

next week.

In light of the appalling reviews of your facility it is not reasonable for me to spend the money on such an establishment. I expect my deposit to be refunded in full.

Colin Fairweather

The message had been sent twenty minutes earlier when Rose had been sealing the chicken in the frying pan.

The email and the phone call had mentioned terrible reviews but all the guests had been glowing in their praise while they'd been here. The Murphys had been so impressed they wanted to come again this season, but Liam had turned them down because he was fully booked. Although now she supposed he wasn't any longer.

With trembling fingers she typed Liam Wood's Chalet into the internet search engine. The first entry was Liam's website but beneath that were several review sites. She clicked on the first one.

At the top was a review from Bryn

but she only skimmed over his complimentary comments because beneath that was the most awful review she'd ever seen! She read through the vitriolic words quickly, unable to believe anyone could be so horrible. Tears began to gather in the corners of her eyes as she read about the uncleanliness of the rooms, the tasteless food and the arrogance of Olympic medallist, Liam Woods.

'Rose,' called Liam. 'Are you in?'

She swallowed. 'I'm in the sitting room.'

'Oh, hi,' he said stepping into the room. 'The guests are having a couple of runs without me so I thought ... hey, what's wrong?'

'Um ... ' Rose wiped her tears away on the sleeve of her jumper.

'Hey,' said Liam softly.

He crouched down by her chair and gently wrapped his arm around her. She leaned into him, smelling the lovely combination of citrus shower gel and the outdoors on his skin. He brought his other arm around her and lightly stroked her back murmuring soothing words into her hair. She wanted to stay there, warm and secure, but she was in his arms under false pretences. It was her who should be comforting him, not the other way around. She pulled herself away from him.

'I'm really sorry, Liam, but something horrible has happened.'

'Whatever it is we can sort it out together. Tell me what's wrong,' he said, his face so close to hers she could see the individual hairs of his stubble. She longed to reach up and trace them along the edge of his jaw.

'There's at least one hideous review about this place on a travel website. One of the guests has seen it and has cancelled. His email indicates that there is more than one bad review out there.'

Liam paled. 'Show me.'

She turned the screen so that he could get a good look. He stayed crouching next to her, not speaking as he read the brutal assassination of his chalet. When he'd finished he scrolled down the site looking at the others. There was a short, sweet review from the newly-married couple but underneath that was another scathing report, mentioning similar problems, namely that the chalet was grubby, over-priced and that Liam was rude to the point of being arrogant. Without speaking he logged onto another site. In all there were six horrible reviews and three good ones.

Liam puffed out a long breath and sank back to sit on the floor. 'This is bad,' he said.

'Yes,' croaked Rose, tears flowing faster than she was able to wipe them away.' I'm so sorry I've let you down. I can work until you find someone else to take my place but I completely understand if you'd like me to leave straight away.'

Liam raised an eyebrow, 'Sometimes you don't make any sense. Why would I want you to leave?'

'It's my fault the rooms aren't clean enough and the food is awful. I've tried so hard but…'

'I suppose you're to blame for my

rudeness and arrogance too?' said Liam, a smile tugging at the edge of his mouth.

'You're not arrogant or rude,' she said quickly.

He tilted his head to one side. 'I try not to be, but listen to me, Rose … ' He knelt in front of her so their faces were at equal height. 'The rooms are spotless and your cooking is delicious. If you left I would be absolutely stuck, so don't even think about it. Whoever wrote those reviews has never been to the chalet.'

'What do you mean?'

'Have you noticed that they all say much the same thing and that they are all posted by 'anonymous'? Another big giveaway that these reviews are fake is there are nine reviews and I've only had five groups since I opened.'

'Oh,' she said, turning back to face the computer. 'Of course. I don't know how I could have missed that. What shall I do?'

Liam ran his hands through his hair. 'The website allows us to write a comment under each review. It probably won't do much good but at least we can point out that there is no evidence to suggest the reviewer has ever stayed here.'

'We can't be the first people this has ever happened to,' said Rose, scrubbing the last of her tears away. 'I can contact the review site owners and see if we can get them taken down.'

Liam nodded. 'I'll call the Murphys. They loved it here but I notice they haven't written a review yet. I'll also offer them next week at a heavily discounted price. It may be enough to persuade them to come, even though it's during term time and they've not long left us.'

Rose nodded. It was good to have a positive, proactive plan, which was why her heart was fluttering wildly. It had nothing to do with Liam's close proximity or his comment that he'd be lost without her — nothing at all.

'What was it you wanted me for?'

'Pardon?' said Liam frowning.

'Earlier, you were looking for me.'

Liam shook his head, 'It's gone out of

my mind. It can't have been important. What's that amazing smell?'

'Coq au vin. It's slow cooking for this evening.'

'Is there enough for us?' asked Liam, standing and stretching out his muscles revealing a slice of taut stomach as he did so. Rose tore her gaze away with difficulty.

'Of course.'

'Fantastic!' he reached down and lightly ran his fingers across her cheek. 'Please don't get upset about the comments about the cooking. You are an amazing cook and I don't know what I'd do without you.'

He turned and left the room, leaving Rose touching her face and wishing she'd been brave enough to do the same to him.

9

Liam paused outside the bar where he'd arranged to meet Sarah. She'd sounded pleased to hear from him, which made his guilt even worse. Over the last week he hadn't been able to get Rose's suggestion that Sarah might be behind his problems out of his head. The whole thing seemed out of character for the fun-loving girl her knew and yet the motive was the most convincing he could think of.

In fact it was the only one he could think of. Nobody else had anything to gain from his business failing, apart from his mum and dad who were keen for him to join the family business. But he refused to go down that line of thought. His parents might want him to join them, but they were always supportive of whatever else he chose to do.

His thoughts turned back to Sarah. Their relationship had been light and fun, both of them understanding that they needed to travel for work. They made no demands on each other and he'd enjoyed the time they'd managed to get together. It was only when he retired from professional skiing that the relationship had changed. She'd decided to retire at the same time and she'd asked him if he'd like to settle down with her in Britain. She hadn't demanded it. It had been more of a suggestion — to see if they would suit each other in the long term.

He'd considered the prospect. She was a lovely person, great looking and enormous fun, but in the end he knew he belonged to the mountain and a nine-to-five in the suburbs of London would have drained the life out of him within weeks. She hadn't seemed overly devastated when he'd told her, only a little sad that their relationship was over. He'd certainly not seen her cry and she'd not begged him to change his mind.

It was a bit weird that she was out here when she'd been so determined to start afresh — and that she was here in particular, when there were thousands of other ski resorts. He was going to have to question her — but gently. If she got wind that he suspected her of foul play when she was entirely innocent, then it would kill any burgeoning friendship and might ruin his relationship with their mutual friends.

He straightened his shoulders and pushed open the door. He spotted her straight away. She was leaning against the bar, checking something on her phone while several men glanced at her, clearly summoning the courage to go over and chat to her.

Liam stopped on the threshold of the room and searched his heart. No, it didn't stir at the sight of her, nor did it leap when she looked up and caught his gaze. Sarah smiled and he made his way over, all the time thinking of the woman who did cause his heart to jump whenever he saw her, but about which he could do nothing.

'Liam,' she said, standing tall. 'Great

to see you,' she dropped a quick kiss against his cheek.

'It's good to see you too. What are you drinking? I'll get these.'

'I'll have a gin and tonic, please.'

He nodded and gave the order to the barman, trying not to wince visibly at the price. Gone were the days when he was flush with money. It was going to be touch and go this month after another couple of cancellations had come in since the first on Thursday, all of them citing the bad reviews as the reason. He had tried to explain the situation but the guests were adamant that they weren't going to pay the prices Liam was demanding for bad service. He'd managed to keep hold of the deposits but that hadn't helped his bank balance.

He rubbed his forehead. Even the promotions he'd run hadn't been a total success. Yes, he'd rebooked all but one of the weeks, probably because that one was so close to Christmas, but he was taking a big hit. Those reduced weeks would barely turn a profit. He couldn't afford for anything else to go wrong.

'How are you enjoying the season?' he asked Sarah as the barman handed over their drinks.

'Do you know, teaching is a lot more fun than I thought it would be? I know I told you I didn't want to be out on the slopes if I wasn't competing but I was wrong.' She smiled. 'How are you finding life out of the competition circuit?'

'Good,' he said. He took a sip of his beer. Interrogating someone was harder than it looked in the movies. 'Seen any of the old gang?'

An emotion he couldn't identify flickered over her face. 'Yes — Paul and Gareth a few times.'

'I bumped into them on the slopes a few weeks ago. They've been training over in the next valley, haven't they? I kept meaning to get in touch but I've been so busy. I guess they're on tour now.'

'Yes, they are.' She bent her head to sip her drink.

'They're coming over to stay at the

chalet for a long weekend with Steve and Mel at the end of January. You should come and stay too.'

'Oh. Thanks, um … that would be good.' A slight frown marred her otherwise smooth forehead.

'Is everything all right?' he asked softly.

'Of course,' she said, looking up at him and smiling brightly. 'Is everything all right with you?'

It was the second time she'd asked him whether things were OK. Was that suspicious or was he reading too much into it?

'Yeah, everything's great.'

They lapsed into silence and Liam took another swig of his beer.

'Look, Liam … ' She paused again. 'I … I've seen some of the reviews posted online.'

He grunted. 'I suppose everyone has.'

She nodded, her face a picture of sympathy.

'They're not written by anyone who's actually stayed at the chalet. Someone's done it to be malicious.' He watched her face but she didn't look guilty or concerned. 'We're in the process of trying to get them taken down but it's slow.'

'Of course, that makes sense. No one who'd met you could ever accuse you of being arrogant.'

'Thanks.'

It depressed him that she believed the other things were true. Did everyone who knew him think he'd keep a chalet in a state of uncleanliness or that he'd employ someone incompetent? Was everyone waiting for him to fail?

He downed the rest of his pint.

'Would you like another?' asked Sarah, moving to get her purse out of her bag.

'No, thank you,' he said.

He wanted to get back to the warmth of the chalet and to sit in the lounge with Rose. He wanted to ask her about her day and watch the expressions that flitted across her face as she talked to him. He hadn't found anything out from Sarah but he didn't want to draw it out any longer.

'OK.' Sarah tossed back the rest of her

drink.

'Shall I walk you home?' asked Liam as they pulled on their bulky jackets.

'No,' she said quickly. 'I mean, no thanks. I'm fine. It's not far.'

'Well, it was good to see you,' he said, puzzling over her strange response. It seemed as if she specifically didn't want him to walk her home.

'Yeah, you too,' said Sarah. She turned and gave him a brief wave as she set off in the opposite direction.

As he trudged back up the hill towards his chalet he tried to recall the whole of their exchange. Sarah had been in turns a bit cagey and at others her normal self. He was fairly sure she was hiding something from him, but it didn't necessarily mean the thing was bad. She certainly hadn't acted like someone who was desperate to get back with him. He was glad when his phone rang and he could stop thinking about Sarah.

'Hi, Mum.'

'Hello, love. How are you?'

He knew immediately that his mum

had seen the reviews. Her tone was too respectful and quiet as if she was enquiring about the death of a loved one.

'I'm fine,' he snapped unfairly. He held the phone away and swore briefly but furiously.

'Don't use language like that, Liam Woods,' said Doreen. He should have known he wouldn't get away with it. His mother had ears like a bat.

'Sorry, Mum. It's been a bad few days but I'm fine, really. I'm guessing from your tone of voice that you've seen the online reviews.'

'I have, darling. Your dad and I were very upset. Have you got rid of her?'

'Who?'

'That chalet girl, Rosa, Rosie … whatever her name is.'

'No, I haven't.'

'What? Are employment rules different out there? Do you need to give her a ridiculous amount of notice? I can come out and help. I'm still pretty good with a mop but I'd need a bit of practice to cook a meal for a large group.'

Liam stopped walking. He could see his chalet from where he stood, the porch light beckoned him on invitingly.

'Did you read all of the reviews?' he asked.

'Yes, I didn't know people could be so rude.'

'And did you believe the bit about me being rude and arrogant?' There was a long pause.

'Of course I didn't, darling, but I thought maybe … well, you know how people get when they're jealous?'

'Mum, someone who's never stayed at my chalet put those reviews on there.'

He heard his mum's outraged gasp.

'Why would someone do such a thing?'

'I don't know.'

'Could it be this Rosa person? I mean you don't know her from Eve. She could —'

'Her name is Rose, and why would she post a review saying she was awful at her job?'

'I suppose, but people do the oddest things. Remember that crazy lady who wanted to work for you so she could have your babies?'

'Rose isn't like that. She's talented, helpful, friendly and kind. She's an amazing cook. I couldn't ask for a better assistant.'

'Oh … ' said his mum.

Then there was an even longer pause. Liam rubbed his forehead. He'd said way too much in his defence of Rose. He knew exactly what was coming next.

'Is she pretty?'

'Mum!' he exclaimed.

Doreen laughed, 'You can't blame me for asking. I'm so desperate for grand-children even that crazy lady is looking promising!'

'Mum! You're being exasperating. Can't you go and pick on one of your other children?'

'I can pick on you all every day.'

'More fool them for living near you!'

Doreen laughed again and Liam continued.

'I saw Sarah this evening,' he said. 'And before you ask, we are not going to get back together.'

'No, I didn't think for a second that you were. You weren't right for each other.'

'I thought you liked Sarah?' he said as he approached the bottom of his driveway.

'I do. She's a good girl but I got the impression you weren't into each other all that much.'

Liam paused at the entrance to the chalet, his hand resting on the door knob. 'You got that impression from her as well, did you?'

'Yes. Oh, I don't mean she didn't like you. I know she did, but not the way I felt about your father when I met him. I haven't upset you, have I?'

'Not at all. That was the impression I had too. I've got to go now, Mum. I've arrived back at the chalet and I don't want to disturb anyone.'

'OK, love. Call me soon, OK? And if anyone writes anything nasty about you again send them to me. I'll sort them out!'

All was quiet inside the chalet. His guests this week were a group of retired couples. They liked to retire early after a good meal and be up as soon as the lifts opened. They were all competent skiers and seemed to want him with them for the novelty rather than being told what to do. Their days were relaxing and not particularly taxing.

He made his way through to the staff area. A loaf of bread was cooling on a wire rack but otherwise the surfaces were spotless. Rose had been working even harder since the bad reviews. The light in her eyes had dimmed a little and he was desperate to put it back, but all the compliments he and the guests gave her failed.

He went through to the sitting room, hoping she would be there warming her feet by the wood burner but the fire was out and the room empty.

He sank slowly into an armchair and rested his head against the cushions. He had to keep reminding himself that Rose was his employee. It was better that she wasn't waiting up for him. Now all he had to do was convince his heart.

10

Rose pulled on her ski jacket. Since the start of the season this was the first week they'd had no guests. After the terrible reviews these guests had cancelled and Liam hadn't been able to refill it. He'd insisted on giving her skiing lessons all week instead — and yesterday he'd declared she was ready for the slopes.

She waddled down to the locker room to find him there.

'I've had good news this morning,' he said, beaming at her.

'You've got guests coming this week after all?'

'No, you don't get off skiing that lightly.'

Her heart skipped a beat. He might think she was scared at the thought of skiing every day, and a couple of weeks ago she would have thought so too, but she was thrilled. Not so much about hurtling out of control down the slopes, but more about spending several days with Liam with no chores on the horizon.

'What is it then?' she asked as she pulled her unwieldy ski boots out of her locker.

'The final travel website has agreed to take the bad reviews down.'

'That's fantastic news. That's all of them now.'

'I know. I'd suggest champagne to celebrate later but my budget won't stretch that far.'

'How about some lemonade instead?'

'It's a date,' he said, grinning and then turning to lift his skis out of his locker.

Rose felt heat rush to her face. She flopped her head forward and took a long time to alter her boot straps. If he guessed how much she wanted a date with her boss she would be absolutely mortified! When she was sure her blush had subsided she looked up again. Really, it was time to put a stop to this debilitating crush. He'd have made a move if he was interested in her in that way. Besides, an international medallist would not be interested in someone like her, who'd spent most of her teenage years helping her mum with household chores.

Hannah had suggested that one of her friends was interested in taking Rose out on a date. She'd text Hannah later and ask her to set it up. Who knows? This mystery man might be the future love of her life. Even if he wasn't, it might help to drive Liam out of her head.

'Where are we going today?' she asked, trying to stand up and flailing helplessly before collapsing back onto the bench. These ski boots were so cumbersome, she didn't know how Liam managed to move around in them so gracefully.

Liam reached down and pulled her to her feet, his hand warm against her cold one.

'We'll go up to the Snake's Head pass,' he said when she was up and balanced. 'It has a lovely long route down, which should be fairly quiet — and the best thing for you is it's not steep.'

'Are you sure you want to spend the day with me? Wouldn't you rather be doing dangerous skiing?' she asked.

'I'll do some dangerous skiing later,' he grinned at her. He really was in a good mood.

* * *

'We need to head to the button lift,' he said when they were standing at the edge of the slope. He waved his pole in the direction they needed to travel. It seemed impossibly far away to Rose but she didn't have time to comment before he slowly started to traverse the slope.

She followed at a comfortable speed marvelling at Liam's controlled technique as he went before her, putting other skiers to shame with his skill.

'Right,' he said when they reached the queue for the lift. 'Getting on these is an art form. You may fall off at first.'

'That will be embarrassing,' she said, looking at the crowd of people around.

He grinned. 'Everyone here will have done the same at some point.'

'Unfortunately that doesn't reassure

me.'

He laughed and all too soon they were at the front of the queue and Liam barked out some instructions. 'Pull the button seat towards you and slide the plastic between your legs. At some point the cord will go tight and you'll be pulled up the mountain. Relax and allow the lift to do all the work. Don't try and ski. You'll be fine, but I'll go behind you just in case.'

The bloke manning the lift shouted something at her in Italian and handed her the button seat.

She tried to put it between her legs but everything was moving so fast.

The seat, half between her legs and half not, began to pull her forward. Her gloved hands scrabbled to try and get hold of something — anything — but to no avail. She landed on her side in a tangle of skis and poles.

Strong arms pulled her to her feet.

'You'd better not be laughing,' she said to Liam as he tugged her back to the start.

'I'm laughing so hard I'm crying,' he wheezed. 'That was spectacularly awful! Let's try again.'

The lift attendant grinned as he handed her a new seat, this time at a much slower speed. With the button wedged securely underneath her she began the slow climb up the mountainside. She didn't dare release her vice-like grip on the cord to take in any of the scenery. Up ahead of her other skiers sailed on as if being dragged up a mountain on a tiny bit of plastic was an everyday normal occurrence. The end was in sight when she lost control of her left leg.

'Keep your legs together,' yelled Liam from behind her.

'I'm trying!' she squealed as her left leg moved further away from the right.

Without conscious effort her left leg lifted into the air.

'Put your ski down,' yelled Liam, laughter lacing his voice.

'It just won't go,' she muttered, frantically waggling her leg to try and regain control but all that did was wave her ski madly around in the air.

She clung on tightly as her left ski dragged ungainly through the snow beneath her. Just when she thought she might make it to the top, her right ski caught and she tumbled to the ground.

Behind her, Liam let go of his own seat and pulled her out of the way of the skiers coming up behind them. He landed on his back next to her, laughing so hard he couldn't speak.

'Are you hurt?' he managed to wheeze.

'Only my pride,' she said.

That set him off again and before long they were both curled up with laughter, tears streaming down their faces.

'What now?' she asked when they'd calmed down enough for her to speak.

'We'll have to climb to the top.'

'What? But it's so far away!'

'It's ten metres at most.'

'Can't we ski down from here?' she pleaded. The amount of effort required to climb those ten metres was going to be incredible.

'We've come up the side of one of the

hardest runs in the whole resort. I don't think you can make it.'

'Why have you brought me up here?' she asked, bewildered.

'The top of the lift leads off to lots of different runs. Come on.'

He pulled himself up seemingly effortlessly.

'Your stomach muscles must be amazing,' Rose blurted out.

Heat rushed over her face as he laughed. What had possessed her to say such a thing?

'Come on,' he said again but this time he held out his hand and pulled her to her feet.

'We climb by digging our skis into the mountain and moving sideways like this.' He demonstrated digging his skis into the snow and climbing a few inches at a time and Rose began to copy him.

The ten metres felt like ten miles as she inched her way to the top, her comment about his stomach muscles playing over and over in her head. She couldn't decide if that comment was too flirty or if he'd take it as friendly. She hoped friendly, because the last thing she wanted was him to think she was interested in him. They lived in such close proximity; it would be unbearable if he pitied her.

'It's this way,' said Liam when they'd finally reached the summit.

He sailed off ahead of her as if the last few minutes had been completely plain sailing instead of agonisingly exhausting! She followed him at a much slower pace over to a wide slope, which fell gently away from the top of the mountain.

'You're right, this does look like my sort of ski run,' she said, watching other skiers meander slowly down.

He grinned. 'Did you bring your phone? There's some fantastic scenery when we get a little further down. We can stop to take some pictures.'

She patted her coat pocket. 'I've got it. Hopefully it survived my fall.'

Liam started to chuckle again. 'I've seen many falls from lifts in my time but I've never seen someone lift their leg quite like that.'

She giggled. 'I really don't know how it happened. I was trying with all my strength to get it to go back down again but it wouldn't obey me.'

He laughed and pushed off slowly.

'Follow me and remember to keep your skis parallel until we turn. Today we're moving away from snow-ploughs towards parallel turns. Can you remember everything I told you yesterday?'

'Yes,' she said.

'You did well on the way down to the lift and this is an easier slope. Follow me and copy what I do. OK? Off we go.'

He slowly dropped away and she followed. They made long C shapes as they swooped sedately down the mountainside.

At first she concentrated solely on where she was placing her feet but gradually she settled into a rhythm and allowed herself to look up from Liam's legs to take in the surrounding view. What she saw took her breath away.

As far as the eye could see were snow-topped mountains reaching up towards a vivid-blue sky, below them bright-green pine trees grew close together, their tops covered in white powder. All she could hear was the swish of her skis over the soft snow. Her soul felt at peace and she understood instinctively why Liam could never work in an office. After being out here, the change in lifestyle would kill him. She doubted she'd ever be able to go back to work in one again either.

After a while Liam slowed and eventually stopped at the side of the slope.

'I'm going to ski down a little and then I want you to come down. I want to check your technique but first . . . ' He pulled a silver flask out of his rucksack. 'Hot chocolate.'

'You brought hot chocolate with you?'

'Yeah.' He grinned and her heart lurched. 'I know how much you love it.'

Oh dear, she was dangerously close to falling very hard for this kind, thoughtful man! He pulled two plastic mugs from his bag and handed them both to her so that he could pour out the drink.

The hot chocolate was made from the

rich, dark stuff that she kept hidden from guests at the top of the cupboard. She let it settle on her tongue before swallowing.

'Do you want to take some photos while we're stopped?' he asked.

She slipped her phone out of her pocket, relieved to see that it had survived her fall intact. She wondered if she could ask him if she could include him in her photograph. She wanted to remember today forever, but she couldn't summon the words and in the end she only snapped a few pictures of the surrounding scenery.

'I understand now,' she said as she slipped her phone back into her pocket. 'Why you want to be out here so much. There's a quality to the silence that you don't get anywhere else.'

He turned to her, his dark goggles pushed up onto his forehead so he could look directly at her.

'Yes, I agree. I don't think you can truly explain to someone how that feels until they experience it for themselves.' He took a sip of his drink. 'What did you do before you came out here?'

'I worked as a temp doing all sorts of work. I kept hoping something would call to me and I would find my niche in life, but nothing ever has.'

'What made you decide to come out here?'

She held the cup to her lips but didn't drink as she debated how much to tell him. In the end she settled for all of it.

'My dad died when I was fifteen. My two brothers are much younger than me and my mum needed me to help her. Oh, she would never ask. She wanted the world for me, she still does, but I could see that she was struggling to work and bring up the boys. I helped her as much around the house as I could and as soon as I was able to, I gave up education and went out to work.

'I don't regret my decision. My brothers are great and we're all very close but I suddenly realised that my twenties were passing me by and I'd never had an adventure. The older of my two brothers went to university and the second one will go next year if he manages to get the right grades, so I'm not needed as much.

'I talked everything over with Mum and it was her idea to get a job abroad. That way I could travel, see a bit of the world and earn some money at the same time. So here I am.'

'Here you are,' he said softly. 'I was lucky I got to you first. Just think, you could be sunning yourself at some bar in Thailand right now.'

She laughed. 'It may be cold up here but it's beautiful. There's nowhere I'd rather be.'

He grinned and held her gaze. For a long moment neither of them spoke and her heart rate picked up a notch.

Liam looked away first. He cleared his throat.

'Do you see down there where it's slightly flat?'

She nodded, unable to speak after that weirdly intense moment.

'That's where the slope crosses with a steeper one. I'll ski to that point and wait for you there. Remember what I said about control. Try to keep both legs on the slope.' He grinned and winked at her before pushing away.

She watched as he quickly made his way down the slope, his moves economical and precise. She'd over-shared and she wished she hadn't. All she'd needed to tell him was that she looking for adventure. He didn't need to know about Dad and the boys. She'd never breathed a word of that to any of her previous employers. She'd never gazed longingly at them either! She shook her head. She needed to get a grip.

She concentrated on her moves as she made her way to Liam's position further down the slope.

'That was good,' he said, when she finally caught up with him. 'I think you could make that better by putting more weight on your outside ski earlier in your turn. I'll show you what I mean as I go down. In case you can't hear me I'll tap my leg so you know when I want you to do it. OK?'

'I need to take my coat off before we

go any further,' she said. 'I'm boiling.'

'Sure, do you want to put it in my rucksack?'

'OK, thanks.'

Underneath her bulky ski jacket she was wearing a more flattering hoody, which didn't make her look like an over-sized snowman.

Liam was just sliding the coat into his bag when two men came down the faster slope that bisected the one they were on. They skied over to Liam, beaming with pleasure.

'Liam,' the taller of the two called. 'It's good to see you.'

'Paul,' he said, looking up from his task. 'And Gareth! I didn't expect to see either of you up here today. Shouldn't you be in . . . ?' He screwed up his face as he tried to remember something.

'The Val d'Isère tournament finished a couple of days ago. We're taking a few days break before we have to travel out to Zagreb,' said Paul.

'Of course,' said Liam. 'How'd you get on?'

‘Gareth came first,’ Paul said, thumping the shorter man on his arm.

‘Congratulations, mate,’ said Liam, smiling.

Gareth grinned back and for a few minutes the men talked about rankings and snow conditions.

Rose switched off and turned to look around her. From where she stood the fast run disappeared over a steep edge while the one she was on meandered peacefully on. A well-worn post indicated the two different directions. She was squinting and trying to make out the names of the villages from the faded writing when she suddenly picked up on their conversation.

‘I saw Sarah the other night,’ said Liam.

‘Yeah, she said,’ commented Paul. ‘She mentioned you’ve invited her to come when we stay in January. It’ll be good to have the old gang back together.’

Rose’s heart lurched uncomfortably at this news. She’d deliberately not asked Liam how his evening with Sarah had gone, even though she was curious to know whether he'd quizzed her on the strange happenings at the chalet. She hadn't wanted to hear him say they'd got back together. She'd become complacent when he hadn't mentioned anything about Sarah, and she'd assumed that would be the end of it.

It was a body-blow to find out his gorgeous ex-girlfriend was coming to visit and that Rose would probably stay in the background cooking and cleaning. She hardly noticed when Gareth and Paul skied away.

'Is everything all right?' Liam asked when it was the two of them again. 'You've gone pale.'

'It's the thought of going down a mountain that steep,' joked Rose as she nodded in the direction Liam's friends had gone. 'Are they friends from your competing days?'

'Yes. We were on a team together. It's not the same as being on, say, a football team. We were sponsored by the same company and so we travelled together and took part in competitions at the same events, although not necessarily against one another. Our winnings not only contributed to our own rankings but also to the team as a whole, so it affected the sponsorship we got. Gareth and Paul are still competing together, which is why it was a surprise to see them here.'

'Do you miss it? The competing. You seemed wistful when you were talking to them just now.'

Liam tilted his head to one side,

'Yes and no. I miss being part of a team but I'd reached the top of my game and there was only one way to go.' He adjusted his helmet. 'I've seen others hang on and start to lose race after race and I didn't want that. Besides — and this might sound strange — I had it in my mind that I wanted to win certain competitions and when I had, the drive went out of me. I wanted to move on to the next challenge, if that makes sense?'

'Yes, it does.'

'And this certainly has been a challenge,' he said, smiling. 'I never thought

I would have to deal with near-bankruptcy, vandals and malicious reviewers.'

'Have you had any further ideas about who might be behind it all?' she asked.

He shook his head. 'None, I'm afraid. I'm convinced it isn't Sarah, though. Right, shall we get on? Can you remember what to do?'

She nodded.

'I'll ski down a bit then and wait for you again.'

He left her standing alone at the edge of the slope. She wanted to ski after him and ask how he knew Sarah was innocent. Was it because he and Sarah were back together? But it was none of her business, so she stayed where she was, the bright winter sun warming her face.

11

Rose pulled on her ski jacket and looked across the kitchen table at Liam, who was busy peeling Brussels sprouts. 'Are you sure you don't want me to stay?' she asked.

'Positive,' he said dropping a peeled sprout into a saucepan and picking up another one. 'This will only take a minute. It's not like I've done much else towards the meal. You're very prepared, so let me do this one thing.'

'You'll remember to put the turkey in the oven when you go out, won't you?'

'Yes,' he grinned and Rose experienced the now familiar flip in her stomach at the sight of it. 'I'll remember and if I don't, I'm sure one of your many notes telling me not to forget will remind me. Now go and enjoy your half-day off. The chalet helpers' Christmas Day ski event is one of the highlights of the season.'

'Everyone knows you've been teaching me. I hope I don't embarrass you by falling spectacularly badly,' she fretted.

'Rose, go.' Liam waved his paring knife in the direction of the door.

'OK, I'm going but remember . . . '

'Rose, I'm not an idiot. I can work the oven and I can remember the turkey. Please don't be late for this.' Rose glanced at the clock, 'Oh no. If I don't get a move on I will be late.'

She heard Liam chuckle as she ran out of the room and down to the locker room. She grabbed her skis and raced as fast as she could to the edge of the slope. After last week's intense daily lessons with Liam she was, if not an amazing skier, at least someone who could stay upright nearly all of the time.

She whizzed as fast as she dared down to the lifts at the bottom of the slope and made her way over to the large group of chalet workers who were taking part in the event, most of whom were wearing Santa bobble hats, the white pom-poms bobbing in a slight breeze.

'You're cutting it fine,' said Hannah, giving Rose a hug. 'Happy Christmas.'

'Happy Christmas to you too. How's things?'

'Lovely. I haven't had to do any work yet and I had the most generous tip from my current guests. How about you?'

Rose squirmed. She'd been up since five preparing Christmas dinner and their guests had yet to make an appearance. When you put it like that the day didn't sound as if it had been fantastic but Liam had been with her and they'd laughed and joked and the time had sped by. He'd even said he'd picked her up a small gift but, if it was OK with her he'd give it to her on Boxing Day, when things had calmed down. Her heart had soared and she'd thought of her own gift for him, hidden under her bed in case he hadn't got her anything. Her crush on Liam was her deepest secret so she couldn't tell Hannah any of that!

'Good so far,' she said instead as they followed the others over to a bubble lift. 'I spoke to Mum and the boys on Skype.

It's a little strange not being with them at Christmas. We've not been apart before.'

'Could they have come out to see you?' asked Hannah as she unclipped her boots from her skis and bent to pick them up.

'Liam did offer but the staff quarters would have been very cramped. Plus, I don't think Mum could afford flights for the three of them,' explained Rose as she copied Hannah.

She still hadn't quite got used to carrying the skis. Others carelessly flung them over their shoulders but Rose was worried about whacking a random passer-by if she did that. So she hefted them along the ground, placing them a few feet in front of her and then walking to catch up with them before repeating the process. It wasn't an easy way to move but it worked for her.

'Couldn't your illustrious employer pay for your family to come over?' asked Hannah, shifting her skis from one arm to the other.

'Oh, I couldn't ask him that! Besides I

don't think the boys wanted to be parted from their friends at this time of year. They're at that age when it's non-stop partying,' said Rose, not wanting to say that there was no way Liam could afford to pay for three flights.

From what she could glean Liam was only just making a profit this year and the disasters that had befallen him had pushed him close to the edge. Sometimes she felt bad taking her salary from him but the one time she had suggested he wait and pay her later in the season he'd vociferously refused. He pointed out how hard she worked and how much he relied on her and wouldn't even consider delaying paying her.

'I'm not keen on these bubble lifts,' said Hannah as they got near to the front of the queue.

'Me neither,' said Rose. 'They always seem to cram too many people into one lift and you end up pressed into some poor person's back for the half an hour it takes to climb the mountain. Or worse you're left facing each other. I was millimetres from some bloke's face on one occasion.'

Hannah laughed, 'That's true. I've got closer to perfect strangers in these things than I have to some of my dates!' Rose giggled. 'Speaking of dates,' said Hannah, as they loaded their skis onto the carrier outside the lift. 'Ed is still keen to go on one with you.'

Rose said nothing as they climbed into the lift and shuffled over to the far side as they waited for other passengers to climb in.

'What do you think?' prompted Hannah when they leaned back against the edge of the lift.

'I don't think so … sorry,' said Rose, pretending to take a great interest in the view outside the lift, which wasn't even remotely interesting as it resembled the inside of a shed.

'Really? Why ever not? He's really cute.'

'Why don't you go out with him then?' asked Rose, trying to deflect attention from herself.

'He's a friend. We've gone past that

sort of thing but I can't understand your reluctance. Ed's fun as well as cute.'

Rose tilted her head to one side. She didn't know how to explain her lack of interest without revealing her unwanted feelings for Liam. She'd originally thought she would go out with Ed and hope that would stop her crush on Liam, but then she'd realised that wasn't fair on Ed. She could hardly go out with one man when her head was full of another.

She was saved by having to give an answer as a couple got on who Rose recognised as friends of Hannah's.

'You remember Eleri and Owen?' Hannah asked Rose after she'd greeted her friends.

'Yes, of course. You were both at the pub quiz last week,' Rose said, smiling with relief. 'Have you been on the Christmas ski run before?'

'Yes,' said Eleri. 'This is our fifth season. We love being out here.'

'Wow,' said Rose, scrabbling around for something else to say to keep the topic of conversation away from Ed and why she didn't want to date him. 'Will you be out next year?'

The couple shared a tender look, 'No, this is our last season for a little while. I'm expecting a baby,' said Eleri.

'Oh, wow!' said Rose again. 'Congratulations.'

'That's amazing news. I'd hug you,' said Hannah, 'but I'm so tightly squashed I can't even move my arms.'

'I'll consider myself hugged then,' said Eleri, laughing.

Rose couldn't help wondering why Eleri was skiing if she was pregnant. What if she fell over and squashed the baby? Rose was worried enough about her phone!

'Are you the chalet girl working for Liam Woods?' asked Owen, peering at Rose from across the lift.

'That's right,' said Rose as the lift wobbled out of the cabin and into the open air.

'How are you finding working for him?'

In Rose's mind, talking about Liam

was as bad as talking about Ed. She'd surely give herself away if she spoke about him at any length.

'He's great to work for,' she said briskly.

'I'd heard he was arrogant,' said Eleri, pushing short black strands of hair back under her Santa bobble hat.

Rose fiddled with the zip on her coat and thought about the hours Liam had spent out on the slopes with her and his patience every time she messed up a turn or something equally simple. She remembered the way he had sweetly arranged the presents under the tree for the young family staying with them at the moment and the way he worried about her working too much even though she was his employee and he was paying her a decent wage.

'I don't know where you heard that from,' she said frostily, 'because he's the least arrogant man I've ever met.'

'I expect you heard that from those horrible reviews,' said Hannah, not seeming to notice that Rose was upset.

'Yeah,' said Owen, 'My boss was gloating over those. He said it served Liam Woods right thinking he could come over here and take up the chalet business when lots of them had been doing it successfully for years. I think he's hoping Liam will fail. He's a bit of an idiot, my boss.'

Rose's fingers had turned cold as Owen spoke. She rubbed her gloved hands together.

'Will it make any difference to your boss if Liam fails?' she asked.

Owen shrugged and gazed out of the lift's windows. 'I'm not sure. He thinks, as do a few of his cronies, that Liam's taken away some of their business. It has been quieter this year and we've had a few weeks where he's had to offer the chalet at a vastly reduced price. That's probably more to do with the fact that he isn't particularly pleasant than anything to do with Liam Woods and his grand chalet.'

Rose nodded and made suitable noises as the conversation moved on and the snow conditions on various runs were discussed. She didn't really pay attention. All she could think about was these men who wanted Liam to fail. If they blamed him for their poor season then was that a powerful enough motive to try and sabotage his business?

If Liam failed to make enough money this year then perhaps he would have to sell his chalet. Local business owners would be in a great position to move in swiftly and buy it. As motives went it was a fairly powerful one.

'Are you all right? You've gone very quiet,' asked Hannah as they neared the top of the mountain.

'Yes, I'm just nervous about slowing you all down,' she lied.

'Rubbish. I've seen you skiing recently and you're almost unrecognisable as the scaredy-cat girl I first saw on the slopes.'

'Hey!' said Rose. 'I wasn't that bad.'

'Yes you were,' laughed Hannah.

The rest of the morning passed in a blur of laughter as Rose whizzed down slopes with her new friends, taking —

and giving — good-natured banter. It wasn't until they were finishing up and starting to head back to their respective jobs that she finally managed to catch up with Owen for a private word.

'Are you still enjoying the season even if your boss is a bit unpleasant?' she asked as they carried their skis towards the waiting bus.

'Yeah, I don't see that much of him to be honest. Eleri and I work hard while we're there so he doesn't have any cause for complaint. He's not very respectful to the guests when he's behind closed doors. Eleri and I find that particularly uncomfortable. If we were coming out next year we wouldn't work for him.'

'What did you say his name was?' she asked. As interrogation techniques it wasn't subtle but Owen was relaxed after spending the morning out in the fresh air and so he didn't query her need to know.

'Robert Turner. You've probably not heard of him, but he was in the Olympics years ago but he came last and never tried again. That's probably why he's against your Liam. Hey, do you think you could get us an introduction to the great man? I've been looking out for him on the slopes but I've not spotted him yet.'

'Yeah, sure. I'll see what I can do. I still owe Hannah an introduction too. Maybe I'll try and get him to come along to one of the pub quizzes.'

'That would be awesome. Do you need a hand with your skis?' Owen asked as they clambered onto the bus.

'Thanks, but I'm OK, you should take care of your pregnant girlfriend.'

Owen laughed. 'She's more likely to take care of me. I've never met a stronger woman.' But he traipsed back off the bus nonetheless leaving Rose to find a seat by herself.

She turned the name Robert Turner over in her mind. She'd never heard of him before. Then again skiing wasn't a sport she'd ever followed before coming out here. She'd only known of Liam because he'd won medals that no British person had previously done and his picture had been everywhere.

Could having sour grapes over a superior chalet cause someone to commit a crime — or was that a preposterous idea?

Whatever the case, she wouldn't mention it to Liam today. She'd let him enjoy Christmas before bringing up her suspicions.

12

Liam arranged the logs in the wood burner and listened to Rose pottering around in the kitchen behind him.

'Are you nearly done?' he called out to her.

'Yes.' She popped her head around the door. 'Would you like a beer?'

'Only if you're having a drink too,' he said, fiddling with a match.

'I was going to have one if you were.'

'Let's go wild then and have one each. I think we deserve it after getting through all that Christmas rush.'

'OK.' Her head disappeared and he heard the satisfying clink of the drinks fridge opening.

He bent down and held the match to the kindling. It caught straight away and he closed the door feeling that buzz of primal satisfaction from starting a fire.

'Here you go,' said Rose, handing him

a beer. 'Do you want any of the leftovers?'

'I couldn't eat another thing,' he said, rubbing his stomach. 'These last few days you've fed us all to bursting point. Please, you should sit down and rest now.'

She sank down onto one of the armchairs and propped her feet on the small footstool.

When he'd bought furniture for the sitting room he'd decided against getting a sofa. It was a small space and a sofa would either have taken up too much of it or been ludicrously small, meaning he'd have been sitting virtually on top of a complete stranger. He'd settled on two armchairs. Now he was cursing his decision. He wanted to slouch on a sofa with Rose curled up by his side. The best he could do was to rest his own feet on the foot stool only inches away from hers.

'I love this wood burner,' said Rose, wiggling her toes happily. 'I'm going to miss its toasty warmth when I leave.'

His heart lurched uncomfortably; he didn't want to be reminded that she'd be gone in a couple of months.

'What are your plans for after the season?' he asked tightly, aware that he needed to be polite even when he didn't want her to go anywhere.

'I'm not sure yet. I'll go home for a bit to see my family and then apply for some other jobs abroad. Hopefully I can get a good reference.' She looked at him and raised her eyebrows.

'Yeah, you're not bad.' He grinned as she nudged his feet off the foot stool. 'I'll give you a great reference, Rose, don't worry about that.'

They sat in comfortable silence for a while. Rose seemed content to watch the flickering flames and he was content to watch the changing shadows as they danced across her face, catching in her small dimple and causing her hair to burn bright gold.

'I can't get my head around the fact that it's Boxing Day,' she said eventually.

'I know what you mean. It can't be Boxing Day if my brother and sister aren't trying to beat me at Cluedo. What would you normally be doing?'

She smiled wistfully. 'On Boxing Day we go to my father's parents' house for dinner. It was a tradition we started when he was alive and then carried on after his death. We eat, watch a film and then play board games too. I always win at Cluedo, by the way.'

He grinned. 'I could nip down to the games room and get the game. I think you'll have met your match in me.'

She laughed. 'Yeah, go on, then — although prepare to be beaten. I always win.'

'OK, but before we do that I wanted to give you your present.' He reached down beside his chair and gathered up the wrapped gifts he'd hidden there earlier.

'Liam,' she said, as she took them from him. 'You said you'd got me one. Now I feel terrible.'

He shifted in his chair and said, 'They weren't expensive...'

She opened the first one.

'I didn't even know they made more than one flavour of hot chocolate. This is great!'

She beamed at him over the small gift box of different flavoured hot chocolates and he felt like a king. He didn't want to think about how long it had taken him to track down that present. He'd had to research her favourite brand and then order the box from Belgium because it wasn't something that was sold in Italy. It was more than he'd ever spent on a simple drink before — but she was worth it.

She put it down on the coffee table and unwrapped the next present.

'Oh! I can't accept this, Liam, really,' she said when she saw it.

'Yes, you can. I hope it fits you all right. I had to guess on the size and I know I didn't do very well on the last one.'

She held the black ski jacket up. 'It must have cost a fortune.'

'I get a hefty discount,' he said, hoping she was concentrating on the jacket enough that she wouldn't notice the blush he could sense creeping up his neck and spreading onto his face. 'I know how much you don't like the jacket you've got. I can't see anything wrong with it but this one is slimline, so hopefully it won't make you feel so much like a snowman.'

She unzipped it and slipped it on. 'I love it,' she said, stroking the arms. 'It will be so much easier to ski with this on.' She quickly took it back off again. 'Wow — it's boiling. Wait here. I'll go and get your present.'

She left the room and he sunk his head into his hands. Every day it was getting harder to act as if he didn't care about her. How soon would it become apparent to everyone that he was in love with her?

He jerked his head back up. Where had that thought come from?

He wasn't in love with her. He'd never been in love before, but he was pretty sure he would recognise the feeling when he felt it. He loved her company, he found her incredibly attractive and his favourite part of the day was whenever he got to talk to her. But that wasn't love, surely?

'Here you go,' she said, coming back into the room and plonking a soft, wrapped present onto his lap. 'As I said, it's not much and it doesn't compete with these lovely gifts but … '

Inside was a dark-blue jumper similar to his favourite one, which had recently developed an un-fixable hole and been consigned to the bin.

'Thank you,' he said quietly. 'I love it.'

She nodded and took a long sip of her wine.

'Shall I … '

'Would you … '

They laughed awkwardly.

'You go first,' she said.

'I was going to suggest that I go and get Cluedo,' Laim said.

'Good idea,' she said, not looking up at him.

'What were you going to say?'

'Oh, it can wait … '

He paused for a moment to see if she was going to elaborate but when she didn't, he got up and went to the games room.

He sighed when he saw the state of it. Rose seemed to spend an inordinate amount of time tidying in here only for it to get messed up by the younger guests almost immediately. Their parents were spending an awful lot of money to come to his chalet and be waited on, but would it really hurt them to put things back in order when they finished?

He heard the sound of guests emerging from the bedrooms so he grabbed the Cluedo and raced back to the staff quarters. Tidying up could wait for tomorrow. As much as he liked this group, he didn't want to get chatting to them when he could be spending time with Rose.

'I found it,' he called through to her from the kitchen. 'Would you like another drink while I'm out here?'

'No, I don't think I will, thanks,' came her oddly stiff response. 'You've got a visitor.'

He turned and saw her standing in the doorway of the sitting room. She was smiling but it didn't reach her eyes. Behind her Sarah emerged, clutching the strap of her handbag and looking equally as strained.

'I think I'll just call it an early night,' said Rose. 'Thanks again for the, um … the … ' she shrugged. 'You know.'

She brushed past him on her way out but she didn't glance up to look at him.

'Sarah.' He sighed, dropping the board game onto the kitchen table. 'What can I do for you?'

'Do you think I could have a drink?' she asked, shifting from foot to foot.

'Of course. Do you want a lager?'

'Yes, please.'

Liam wasn't used to Sarah being so polite. It was unnerving. He flipped open the bottle and handed it to her.

'Can we go … ?' she nodded her head towards the sitting room, her gaze quickly flicking towards Rose's closed bedroom door and away again.

'Sure.'

Sarah led the way.

'Well, this is cosy,' she commented as she lowered herself into Rose's seat.

He wanted to tell her she couldn't sit

there but as the only alternative was the floor, he knew he was just being ridiculous. A chair didn't belong to someone, especially when they weren't actually sitting in it.

He sat opposite Sarah but he didn't lean back. If he gave her the impression he was in a hurry hopefully she would leave, and his evening with Rose could be salvaged.

'I wanted to tell you something,' said Sarah, running her fingers along the strap of her handbag and looking anywhere but at him.

'Oh,' said Liam, hoping against hope she wasn't going to say she wanted them to get back together again. It was the absolute last thing that he wanted — but he also didn't want to hurt her feelings.

Not when he was experiencing unrequited love himself.

'I had a whole speech planned but now I can't say it,' she said, her gaze fixed on the flames dancing in the wood burner.

'Best say something,' said Liam uncomfortably.

‘Then I won’t sit here worrying about what it is.’

She took a gulp of her beer, ‘I have a confession to make.’

Liam’s heart stopped. Was she about to tell him she’d been behind the nasty pranks? Had she done it to be funny? As a team, they’d often played jokes on one another but never anything that had actually hurt.

Maybe she’d felt she’d gone too far with the reviews. The pranks did seem to have stopped since they’d been taken down from the websites but he was constantly waiting for the next thing to befall him.

‘It’s about Paul,’ she said into the silence.

Liam had been so convinced she was going to say something else that he couldn’t get his head around her statement. What did Paul have to do with anything?

‘Paul came to visit me over the summer,’ she said, still not taking her eyes from the fire.

He waited for her to continue but when she didn't his imagination ran away with him. Why would Paul want to hurt his business if they were in this together? He and Paul had always been great friends. He searched his memory, looking for a moment when he'd annoyed Paul so much that his friend might have become his enemy.

'I'm sorry, Liam, neither of us meant to hurt you,' Sarah turned her face away from the fire and looked directly at him for the first time. Unshed tears glistened in her eyes.

'Yes, well . . . ' said Liam, not knowing where to look. He'd never been able to cope with tears but he had to stand his ground. He needed to find out why they had attacked his business, and in doing so, attacked him too. 'Why did you do it?' he asked gruffly.

Sarah couldn't have looked more shocked. 'I . . . well, he . . . I think . . . well, he's very good-looking I suppose. Not that you aren't, obviously, but I always felt you and I were . . . not quite right.

But with Paul ... ' She sighed and even through the tears he could see a light of happiness in her eyes. A light he'd never seen there before.

He rubbed his forehead, 'Start from the beginning, Sarah. What is it about you and Paul?'

Sarah looked at him oddly. 'We've been dating for a while. Paul wanted to tell you straight away but I made him wait until we were sure our relationship was going to last. I didn't want to hurt you unnecessarily. I was going to tell you the last time we met, but I chickened out. Why? What did you think I was talking about?'

A wave of relief rushed through Liam, to the extent of weakening his knees and causing him to flop back in his chair.

'I thought you were going to say you and Paul had written those reviews on that website for a joke!' he said after a few minutes of silence.

'Really! Why on earth would Paul and I do such a thing?' said Sarah indignantly.

'I don't know. That's why I was so

shocked.'

'Oh, you're not upset about Paul and I then?'

'No,' he said laughing. 'You were right about us — we weren't quite right, but you and Paul ... I can see that's a good fit. You'll make each other happy.' He grinned at her and she smiled back.

'Phew, that's a relief!' Her handbag strap fell down her arm as she relaxed into the chair. 'I thought I should tell you before we come to stay at the end of January.'

'Yeah,' he said although he wished she hadn't called round to do it. A text message would have been sufficient.

His nights with Rose with nothing to do were very rare and Sarah's arrival had spoilt things. It could be a month before they had time again.

Even though he didn't offer Sarah another drink she took an age to finish the one she had. She seemed to think he wanted to hear all the gossip from this year's racing circuit.

He nodded politely but didn't ask any

questions which might prolong her chat. Had she always talked this much? he wondered as she finally tipped the last of her drink into her mouth.

He supposed they hadn't been alone much when they were a couple as they were always surrounded by friends on the circuit. If they had been together like this more often, their relationship probably would have floundered much earlier on. He didn't really enjoy gossiping about people, even if most of the news was friendly.

Finally she was ready to leave.

'It was so good to see you, Liam,' she said as she laced up her boots by the back door. 'Thank you for being so understanding.'

She enveloped him in a hug and he gave her a brief squeeze in return. It amazed him to think she had considered, even for a moment, that he would be upset about her moving on with someone else. It hadn't occurred to him.

Now if Rose announced she was dating someone …

His hands curled involuntarily and he focused on relaxing them. It wasn't his place to get jealous. It wasn't as if Rose had ever given him reason to suspect she might be interested in him. For all he knew, there could be a guy waiting for her in Britain.

When he'd locked up behind Sarah, he stood in the kitchen looking at the clock. Sarah had been there the best part of an hour giving him a rundown of everyone's business. The chances of Rose still being awake and wanting to play a board game with him or just sit and chat were very slim.

He made his way over to her bedroom door. It was impossible to tell whether her light was on or off. He debated switching the hall light off so he could see, but decided she'd consider it creepy if she found him standing outside her bedroom in the dark.

He shook his head. He was acting like a crazy man. He would let Rose rest in the peace and quiet of her room. It wasn't her fault he was falling for her and she needed her sleep to cope with tomorrow. It would be a long day again.

He wandered over to his bedroom and hung his new jumper in his wardrobe.

It was only when he was drifting off to sleep that a thought occurred to him.

If Sarah wasn't behind those reviews, then he was no closer to finding out who was.

13

Rose cut around the edges of the dish so that the pastry finished on the lip rather than dangling over the side. Then she neatly pressed around the outside to seal the pastry.

'Hey,' said Liam, rushing through the kitchen trying to tug a sock on as he went. 'Are you sure you don't want to come with us?'

'Thanks, but I've got to get this pie on.'

'You don't have to cook for us this weekend. These are my friends, not proper guests. They'll be happy with a takeaway.'

'I like cooking,' she said, smiling at him as he hopped about the room. It would be far quicker if he sat down to put on his clothing. 'I went for a long ski yesterday with Hannah and everyone.'

Was she imagining it or did he look

disappointed? Surely not!

She was the only one staying in the chalet this weekend who had never skied competitively. If she came with them they'd all have to wait for her. They'd very quickly become bored. Liam would have a much better time if he skied wherever he wanted and didn't have to babysit her.

'Come out with us tomorrow,' insisted Liam.

'Hmm,' she murmured non-committally, moving the pie to the back of the kitchen counter and getting out the chopping board.

'OK, I'll see you later,' he said.

For a mad second she thought he was going to kiss her goodbye, but he gave her a brief wave and left.

She leaned against the kitchen counter, her heart hammering. What was wrong with her?

When was her body going to catch up with the idea that he wasn't interested in her?

She put her head in her hands and groaned. The problem was that recently she'd begun to think that he might actually like her — even if not as much as she liked him, then at least more than as a friend.

It had started with the thoughtful Christmas gifts. Although he'd insisted he'd got the jacket heavily discounted it was the fact that he'd seen that she was uncomfortable in her bulky jacket and thought to get her a better one that touched her heart. Then there had been the hot chocolates. He'd obviously taken note of the brand she liked and had gone one better by buying her a selection of different flavours. He must have searched for it because she'd hadn't found anything similar in the local supermarkets.

On Boxing Day she'd been gearing up to ask him if he'd like to go out for a meal or something when Sarah had arrived. Sarah with her lovely, long blonde hair and her soft-looking skin had wanted to talk to Liam privately.

Rose had wanted to shut the door in the beautiful woman's face but Sarah had never done anything to hurt Rose so she knew she couldn't. Besides if Liam still loved Sarah, then it wasn't fair for Rose to interfere.

Coward that she was, she'd been unable to ask Liam what Sarah had wanted the next day and Liam hadn't shared the information.

He'd seemed lighter and happier after her visit so maybe they were back together. Rose wanted him to be happy, she just would have preferred it if she was the one putting the smile on his face.

Now there was this weekend and everything was confusing. The house had been full of laughter since the first of his friends had arrived. Liam had tried to involve her, but she didn't want to risk seeing him with his arms around Sarah and so she'd cowardly kept to her part of the chalet, only venturing out when everyone else was on the slopes.

Sarah wasn't sharing Liam's room and last night he had definitely come back to his own bedroom alone …

Rose smacked herself on the forehead. She must stop this obsessing. When

Liam came back she would ask him outright whether he and Sarah were back together. There was nothing wrong in that. All she needed to do, in the hours they were out on the slopes, was to plan how she was going to ask him without looking weird.

When she'd chopped all the vegetables and prepared an apple crumble for dessert she took herself off to the sitting room and sat down to phone her mum.

'How's Liam?' asked her mum after they'd exhausted all other topics.

'He's good. He's got his friends staying this weekend so it's a little more relaxed than normal.'

'Has he noticed how beautiful you are yet?'

'Mum! What makes you say such a thing?'

Her mum laughed, 'It's always, 'Liam this' and 'Liam that'. I'm guessing that he's become more to you than just an employer.'

Rose sighed. It was no use hiding things from her mum. 'I do like him a lot but he has an ex-girlfriend who's staying here at the moment. They still seem very close so don't get your hopes up.'

Her mum paused, 'You'll be off soon anyway, won't you? There's lots of the world out there for you to see, birds in the bush and all that.'

Rose smiled at her mum's words; she was always getting her sayings muddled. 'Yes, you're right, and I fancy somewhere warm this time.'

She listened while her mum talked about possible destinations, but for the first time since Rose had come up with the idea to travel she found that her heart was torn. She wanted to see the world, but she wanted to stay with Liam too.

* * *

Later Liam insisted she dine with him and his friends and she couldn't think of a reason why not that didn't make her seem very rude.

She sliced the chicken and mushroom pie in the kitchen, wishing she were somewhere else. What if Liam and Sarah were holding hands at the dinner table? She didn't think she'd be able to hide her look of horror.

She put wide slices of pie on each plate but she left the mash and veg in serving dishes so that everyone could help themselves. When there was nothing else to be done, she began to put everything on large trays.

'Is everything ready?' asked Liam coming in to help her carry it through to the dining table.

'Yep, if you could grab the tray with the plates that would be great. Did you have a good day out?' she asked as he moved some plates around to get a better balance on the tray.

'Yeah, it was great. We're going to spend the whole day out tomorrow, probably skiing over to the next valley. Will you join us for some of the run? I'd like you to see the Val di Giocobbella. Most of the runs are further down the mountain than the valley we're in now and are lined with trees so it's prettier.

There are lots of runs you'd find suitable. I can come with you and keep you company if they're too tame for the others.'

'That's kind of you but I don't want to take you away from your friends,' she said concentrating fiercely on the tray in front of her.

Out of the corner of her eye she saw him shrug, 'I get to see them all the time whereas you ... '

He left the sentence unfinished as he picked up the tray. Rose's heart began to beat erratically. Was he implying he wanted to spend time with her? She shook her head. No, he wasn't implying it — he was stating it explicitly. Her hands trembled as she picked up dishes overflowing with honey-roast carrots and buttery mash.

'If you're sure then I would love that,' she said.

He looked up from the plates and caught her eye. For a long moment the only sound Rose could hear was her own breathing.

A slow smile crossed his face. 'That's

great.'

She followed him to the dining room. The volume of chatter rose as she and Liam approached.

'You met everyone earlier,' Liam said as he handed out the plates, 'But to recap … the redhead is Gareth, he's the snowboarder who's won competitions for his tricks in the halfpipe. Steve and Mel,' he waved a spoon in the direction of a dark-haired couple at the end of the table, 'are the old folk of the group. They retired from professional skiing a couple of years ago. Their skiing is a little rusty as you'll see tomorrow.'

The group laughed and Mel threw a crumpled serviette at Liam's head. 'Don't listen to him Rose, we're better than him any day of the week.'

'You've met Sarah already and this guy, with the hipster beard, is Paul.'

Rose smiled at them all and settled into her seat as they all complimented her on her cooking.

Sarah, she noticed, was sitting very close to Paul and she lightly touched his wrist whenever she spoke. Rose glanced at Liam to see whether he was getting annoyed by this display of affection but he seemed in very good spirits. A tension she didn't know she'd been carrying around with her slowly seeped out of her bones. It was obvious, even to her, that Sarah wasn't interested in Liam.

Liam poured Rose a glass of wine and she found herself smiling a lot as the meal progressed. Liam was single and he wanted to spend the day with her tomorrow, not because he was worried about her skiing ability but because he wanted to keep her company. She almost floated to the kitchen to fetch the crumble when everyone had finished the first course.

'Where did you learn to cook like this?' asked Sarah, as she handed over her bowl for a second helping of the pudding. 'I even burn pasta!'

Rose laughed. Now that she wasn't worried Sarah was going to take Liam away from her she had realised that the young woman was a lot of fun. 'My dad died when I was quite young and my mum went out to work. She was often so exhausted in the evening that I took over the cooking. It was that or starve.'

Sarah reached over and squeezed Rose's hand. 'You have my complete admiration. Also, will you come and live with me so that I can eat like this every day?'

'You wouldn't believe the amount of people who want to steal Rose away from me,' said Liam. 'I've had to fight off all my guests because I really won't allow it. Even if I have to chain her to the house, she's not leaving!'

Rose's heart fluttered at his pronouncement.

'Whatever he's paying you, I'll pay you double,' said Mel, winking at Rose.

'Don't listen to them,' said Liam waving his fork around. 'Their chalet is in a horrible place. Really, really horrible. You wouldn't enjoy living with them at all.' He shuddered theatrically.

'There are beautiful lakes within a two-minute walk of Mel's chalet. You can go ice-skating on them,' said Gareth grinning wickedly.

'You're not helping, Gareth,' said Liam and everyone laughed.

'You mustn't wash up,' said Sarah as Rose went to gather up the plates after they had all finished second helpings of the crumble. 'Paul and I will do the dishes.'

'I don't mind. Most of it goes in the dishwasher anyway,' said Rose shyly.

'Nonsense,' said Gareth. 'Let the two love.birds do whatever they want in the kitchen. They can have a bit of time by themselves while we all play pool.'

That answered that question, then. Paul and Sarah were definitely a couple. She shot a quick glance at Liam and found that he was watching her. He winked and she grinned back.

'If you insist,' she said. 'I would love to play pool. I haven't played since I came out here.'

'That's a crime when you've got a table here. Shall we make up a team and play against Steve and Mel? Liam can adjudicate,' said Gareth, helping Sarah to gather up plates. 'Steve always cheats,' he mock whispered.

Liam's friends left the room, laughing and joking as they took the empty dishes to the kitchen.

'Are you sure about me playing pool?' she asked Liam when they were alone. 'I feel a bit like I'm skiving.'

'It's a weekend off,' said Liam smiling. 'I don't want you to feel you have to wait on my friends and I know they're not expecting it.' He fiddled with his serviette. 'Steve and Mel are looking for a chalet girl. Their last one left last week after deciding the snow wasn't for her. I'm sure they would pay you double if you're interested.'

Rose's heart dropped. 'Do you want me to go?' she asked quietly.

'No!' he said sharply. 'I just thought you should know there's more money to be had out there. I was joking before, their chalet is in the most beautiful place. I feel guilty paying someone as talented as you as little as I do, but I really don't want you to go.'

'I don't want to leave,' she said softly.

'Good,' he said and for the second time that evening he held her gaze. Slowly, infinitely slowly, he moved his hand across the table towards her. The air around her seemed to tremble and shimmer. Without thinking she moved her own hand towards his.

'Ready to become a winner, Rose?' came Gareth's voice from just outside the dining room.

Liam jumped and pulled his hand back.

Rose cleared her throat. 'I'm ready.'

Whatever had been about to happen was clearly over before it had begun. Rose's body fizzed with anticipation as well as disappointment; there were weeks left with Liam. Something was bound to happen in that time.

In the end Gareth proved to be a funny but fairly hopeless partner. They lost repeatedly until he admitted defeat and allowed Liam to take over. Paul and Sarah didn't make a reappearance and, although Rose searched Liam's face, he didn't seem remotely bothered. As the night wore on she became tired and when the hot tub was suggested she made her excuses to go to bed.

Snuggled under the thick duvet, she replayed the evening. Twice it had seemed as if Liam was on the verge of kissing her. If they'd been on their own this weekend, would it have happened? She wiggled her toes. If he kissed her she would make it very clear she wanted to kiss him back.

She rolled over onto her side and picked up her diary from her side table. Flicking through it, she realised there weren't that many days in the next eight weeks where she and Liam would be left on their own. She held the diary to her chest. If she wanted to be alone with him, then she would have to create time. She fell asleep dreaming of ways to make it happen.

14

Liam woke to the smell of cooking and the sound of feminine laughter. He was glad Rose was getting on well with his friends but he wished they would all disappear.

Last night he'd been so close to kissing Rose and from the look in her eyes she'd wanted him to. As much as he'd wanted things to run their natural course, he had to admit they'd both had more to drink than normal. Perhaps it was just as well they were interrupted. Life would be awkward if she realised the extent of his feelings but didn't return them.

He levered himself out of bed and rummaged around in his wardrobe for some fresh clothes. He pulled out the jumper Rose had bought him for Christmas and without thinking too much about his motives, he slipped it on.

Outside his bedroom the kitchen was a

hive of activity. Sarah was watching over a pan of sizzling sausages while Gareth buttered toast and Rose was turning thick rashers of bacon on the grill.

'You're up late,' said Gareth. 'A few months out of training and you're already going soft.'

'Ha, it was the late night in the hot tub. How come everyone else is looking so cheery?'

'I tell you, mate, you're going soft,' said Gareth, grinning. 'Where do you want me to put this toast, Rose?'

'If you don't mind taking it all through to the dining room that would be great, thanks, Gareth. Everything's nearly ready. Liam, could you take the coffee and tea through, please?'

She smiled at him briefly before turning her attention back to the grill.

He nodded and began putting the teapot and coffee jug onto a tray.

'Liam!' called Paul urgently from somewhere in the chalet. 'You need to come!'

Paul sounded panicked. Leaving the

drinks tray Liam shot out of the kitchen.

'Where are you?' he called back.

'Here,' said Paul, standing at the top of the stairs that led down to the locker room. 'You need to come downstairs.'

With a mounting sense of dread Liam quickly followed Paul downstairs. What could have happened now? The locker room was padlocked every night so surely all his pipework was safe.

He staggered as his feet hit the ground floor. The scene inside the locker room was his worst nightmare. The outside door of the locker room was hanging off on its hinges and expensive equipment was lying, broken and snapped, all around the room. His friends' expensive equipment. Equipment he was now honour-bound to replace with money he didn't have!

'Oh, my God!' said Sarah, coming into the room behind him. 'My skis …' she wailed, taking a step towards them.

'Don't touch anything,' said Paul. 'Let's go up to the main house and call the police.'

Sarah disappeared up the stairs but Liam didn't move. This was a disaster. He was ruined!

'Come on,' said Paul, gently taking his arm. 'You need to phone the police.'

He nodded slowly but he still couldn't take his eyes of the carnage. 'Who would do such a thing?' he asked gruffly.

'I don't know, mate, but we're not going to get any answers standing here staring at it. Let's go and break the news to the others.'

Liam climbed the stairs with legs made of lead.

By the deathly silence coming from his friends, huddled in the lounge, Sarah had already broken the news. He was grateful. He didn't think he could find the words to tell his friends that hundreds of pounds worth of damage had happened to their equipment while it was in his house.

'I called the police,' said Sarah quietly.

'Thanks,' muttered Liam.

'How bad is it?' asked Steve.

'It's very bad. I didn't get a chance to

go through it all but it looks as if everyone's stuff has been damaged. What do you think, Paul?' He looked at his friend, who had sat down next to Sarah and taken her hand in his.

'There was only one locker still locked. Every other one had been ripped open and its contents pulled out,' said Paul soberly.

'Thank goodness most of the lockers were empty,' said Sarah.

Liam's legs turned to rubber as he realised just how bad that scene would have been if proper paying guests' equipment had been destroyed like that. He didn't think he'd have been able to survive the negative reviews that would have followed. As it was he was going to have a hard time coming back from this, if he even could.

'Does anyone want breakfast while we wait for the police?' Liam asked tiredly. He didn't think he could eat a thing but perhaps the others were hungry. Why was someone doing this to him?

'It would be a shame for all that food

to go to waste,' said Paul practically. 'I'll go and help Rose bring it through to the table.'

Liam followed the others into the dining room. The toast was already there, going cold in the centre of the table. Nobody reached to take a piece. Paul brought in the sausages and bacon and Rose followed with a tray of fried eggs, her face looking pinched and drawn. She smiled sympathetically as she passed him but she didn't join them. After a while she returned with fresh pots of tea and coffee and some warm toast before heading back to the kitchen.

Talk over breakfast was very subdued. Liam managed to force down a few rashers of bacon and an egg but he felt as though it was lodged in his throat, no matter how many cups of tea he drank to try and wash it down.

The police arrived soon after they'd finished eating. He and his friends had lived and worked in Italy so their Italian was reasonable enough. Even so, there really wasn't much to report.

The damage could have been done from any point after six in the evening yesterday until Paul went down there around eight this morning. Nobody had heard anything or noticed anything untoward. They'd been together all evening until they'd gone to bed.

The police questioned Liam separately and he told them about the other things that had happened to him since he'd started the chalet project. They nodded sympathetically but he didn't think he'd convinced them that there was an active campaign against him.

A wide pit of despair had opened in his stomach as the police inspected the scene and took some fingerprints. He could tell from their comments and the lacklustre way they moved around the room that they didn't hold out much hope of catching whoever was responsible. So many people had come through the locker room that fingerprints were almost useless and without CCTV cameras, there was no other evidence.

Now he'd had a chance to calm down,

he realised his insurance would pay out for the damaged equipment. Such a large claim would increase his premiums but in the short term it was better than handing over cash he didn't have.

After the police had gone, he took his friends down to take a look at the damage. Not one item had been left untouched. Skis were snapped, goggles smashed, hats and gloves squashed into the dirt on the floor. He knew none of his friends would be able to use the clothes again no matter how clean they got them — they now felt violated.

'Why is that locker untouched?' asked Sarah, pointing to the only one to remain closed.

'I don't know,' shrugged Liam.

'Is there anything in it?' she asked.

'It's Rose's,' he said quietly. 'Perhaps whoever destroyed everything knew that and realised her equipment would be cheap. If that's true then it would narrow down the list of suspects.'

'Hmm,' said Gareth sceptically.

'What's that supposed to mean?'

demanded Liam, anger flaring up at his friend's tone.

Gareth leaned against the wall, one of his broken skis clutched in his hand. 'I like the girl, don't get me wrong, but doesn't anyone else find it odd that her stuff wasn't touched?'

'Don't be absurd,' said Liam, looking around at the rest of his friends for support but none of them would meet his eye.

'She went to bed before all of us,' Sarah said.

Gareth nodded. 'Yeah, she did. Hours before us, in fact.'

'So you're saying that Rose, who incidentally is tiny, came downstairs after pretending to go to bed, smashed the padlock, broke all of the skis and then went to bed as if nothing had happened. To what end?' Silence reigned. 'Seriously, Gareth, what on earth would be her motive?'

Gareth shrugged. 'I don't know but didn't you get all those weird girls getting in touch after seeing your picture in the paper? Could she be one of those?'

'I repeat, what would she gain from doing this?' asked Liam coldly.

'Don't turn on us, Liam,' said Sarah softly. 'We're your friends. No one is blaming Rose, we're just pointing out that it's a little odd that these strange things are happening to you since she's been around.'

'Rose is not responsible,' he ground out. No one spoke. Somewhere high above him he heard the sound of the front door close.

Rose had left the building.

15

Tears blinded Rose as she raced away from Liam's chalet, Gareth's cold assessment of her ringing in her ears. She stumbled as she reached the end of the driveway and she fell onto her side, wetting her jeans as they made contact with the snow. She pulled herself upright and brushed the ice from her leg. She wasn't going to return to the chalet to change. She couldn't face looking at Liam's face and seeing the suspicion in his eyes.

A bus was pulling into a nearby stop and she jogged towards it. With no thought as to where she was going she boarded and made her way to the back. By the time she was sitting, tears were flowing rapidly down her face. She brushed them away with the back of her hand.

What a nightmare!

If Liam believed, or even suspected

for a second, that she was guilty of doing those horrible things then she would have to find another job. A sob escaped her at the thought of leaving him but she knew she'd have to. Even if Liam said he didn't suspect her, Gareth had sown the seed of doubt and he wouldn't trust her from now on.

The bus reached the town without her noticing any of the passing scenery and she piled out with the other passengers. She had no direction and she wandered miserably from shop to shop picking up merchandise without really seeing what she was holding before putting it back on the shelves with a desultory thud. She'd only come out with a handful of coins and by the time she'd trudged disconsolately around all the shops she realised her stomach was rumbling madly. She hadn't felt like breakfast hours ago but now she was starving. She scratched her nose and realised her fingers were icy; she'd come out without her gloves on.

Her legs took her to the cafe she'd been to with Liam after her first skiing lesson all those months ago. She remembered the thickness and comforting warmth of their hot chocolate and the welcoming blaze of their fire. She let herself into the bustling room and stood for a moment, letting the warm air soak into her skin.

'I was hoping you'd come in here,' said a voice from behind her.

She turned and found Liam leaning against the wall, a half drunk pint of lager next to him.

She burst into tears.

'Hey,' he said, pulling her towards him and enveloping her in his arms. 'Don't cry.'

He brought a hand up to her hair and stroked it gently as she sobbed into his shoulder.

'You're freezing,' he murmured as his thumb brushed her cheek. 'Would you like a hot chocolate?'

She nodded into his chest but she didn't let go, 'I didn't do it!' she gasped.

'Of course you didn't,' said Liam, his fingers entangling in her short hair.

'But the others all think … '

'No, they don't. Gareth was upset and didn't know what he was saying. When Paul pointed out how much strength was needed to break that door and trash all that stuff, everyone agreed it couldn't possibly be you. It didn't cross my mind for one second that you were responsible.'

For some reason this statement made Rose cry even harder. Liam tightened his grip and she stayed in the comforting circle of his arms until her sobs subsided. 'Sorry,' she said eventually. 'I don't know why I'm crying so much.'

'It's the shock. Look ... a table's become free. Sit down and I'll get you a hot chocolate — if you promise not to disappear again.' She nodded. 'Do you promise?' His eyes were creased with concern.

'Of course,' she said. 'I'm sorry for adding to the stress of your morning by running away. I couldn't face everyone after hearing what Gareth had to say.'

'Gareth's well-meaning but sometimes he can be a bit of an idiot and he speaks without thinking. He was mortified when he realised you must have heard what he said.'

Rose watched Liam make his way to the counter as she sat down in a snug corner close to the roaring fire. She couldn't believe that Gareth really was mortified. From what she'd heard, he was pretty convinced Rose was guilty. He'd probably backed down when Liam had protested her innocence. Rose knew she wasn't guilty but it did beg the question, if it wasn't her, then who had damaged all that expensive equipment?

Liam returned with steaming mugs of hot chocolate and two large paninis, melted cheese oozing over the sides of the bread.

'What are the others doing for lunch?' she asked as he emptied the tray onto the table.

Liam sank into the chair opposite her and rubbed his face with his hand.

'They aren't able to ski today so they've borrowed the car to go to Turonia. They're going to look for replacement skis and have lunch there.'

'What about you? How will you ski?'

'I've got several pairs. None of them are as good as the ones I lost but I can't afford to replace them right now.' His lips twisted.

'Oh, Liam,' said Rose sadly.

He leaned his head back into the cushion of the chair. 'I'm not going to lie, Rose. This has hit me hard.' He rubbed his hand over his face again. 'It's not so much the loss of the skis, although that is obviously bad. It's the fact that someone out there hates me enough to do such a thing.'

Liam's shoulders sagged and his mouth turned down at the corners. Rose didn't know what to say to make it better; there probably wasn't anything. She fiddled with the sleeve of her jumper for a moment.

'What did the police say?' she asked.

Liam huffed out a laugh.' They were sympathetic but they don't see any hope of catching the people responsible.'

Rose picked up her panini and took a

bite. Warm cheese mixed with salty ham and juicy tomato hit her tongue and for a moment she couldn't think of anything else apart from finishing her sandwich. After several mouthfuls she put it down again as a plan began to form in her mind.

'We need to find out who's responsible,' she said. 'Then we can stop them.'

Liam put his own sandwich down, 'That's my thinking too, but I don't want you involved.'

'Why not?' she asked indignantly.

'Did you see the locker room?'

She shook her head. She'd been on her way down when she'd heard Gareth's accusation.

'It was a real mess,' said Liam. 'An angry mess! Whoever was responsible was strong and they were methodical in the destruction. It's a huge escalation from nasty reviews or tampering with water pipes. I don't want you getting hurt.'

He returned his attention to his sandwich, a determined frown across his brow. Rose saw she was going to have to be careful.

'I don't want to get hurt either,' she agreed. 'But two heads are better than one. And I have no intention of confronting anyone or doing anything heroic, truly.'

Liam looked up from his sandwich. 'You may not want to get hurt but it could happen anyway. Look at the locker room — I'd deadlocked it and used a bolt, and the person responsible still managed to get in. He or she is determined to get me. I don't want you getting in the way of that because goodness knows what they'll do next —' He was arguing, but there was less heat in his words. Rose could tell from the set of his shoulders that she was winning.

'Do you have a pen on you?' she asked, determined to be involved.

He frowned at the change in conversation, but dug around in his pocket and pulled out a ballpoint. She took it and smoothed out a napkin.

'Who wants you to fail?' she asked.

Liam spread his hands. 'I really don't know.'

'We know some of the locals are against you,' she said. At the top of the napkin she wrote locals. 'And I'm not ruling out Sarah.'

'I don't think it's her,' said Liam and Rose thought that he may not realise it but he wasn't arguing about her involvement anymore.

'She may not have an obvious motive but you can't deny she's had opportunity. Anyone else?'

'Anyone staying at the chalet last night had the opportunity,' Liam pointed out.

Rose nodded and wrote guests under Sarah's name. Then after a moment's consideration she wrote her own name.

'I've told you I don't think it was you,' Liam protested.

'I know but if I've put Sarah's name down then I think I should add my own. Who else? Did you anger someone during your racing days? Someone who might want revenge for you winning races they thought they should have won?'

'There's always rivalry between teams but it's all fairly good-natured. I can't think of anyone, but then I can't think of a single reason anyone would want me to fail either.'

'Let's start with these locals, then. We know they have a reason to be against you. No, don't pull that face. I know you don't agree that it's a strong enough motive, but we've got to start somewhere. This has to stop.'

'I wasn't pulling a face because I disagree with you. The locals do seem like the most logical place to start but I don't see how we're going to go about it. It's not like I can knock on their front door and say, 'Hey, do you hate me? And did you smash up my locker room?' I certainly can't go to the police and accuse anyone with no proof.'

Rose laughed. 'I see what you mean.' She reached over and picked up the remains of her sandwich. She chewed thoughtfully for a moment then sat up straight. 'I know! Why don't you come to the pub quiz on Sunday? The only thing is, it could be a little awkward because the new guests will only have been with us at the chalet for a day.' She shook her head while she thought. 'You could always come for the second half.'

Liam scratched his nose. 'Isn't it Bryn again this week? I'm pretty sure it is because this is one of the cancelled weeks and they were thrilled at getting another week at such a discount. I'm sure he and his wife won't mind me coming out earlier, they're pretty flexible, but why do you want me to come? Isn't your team full already? And my general knowledge is pretty poor. I'm only good at sport.'

'Hannah really wants to meet you, as do Owen and Eleri. Do you remember me telling you about them? She's the pregnant skier. I met them on Christmas Day. We'll form a team with them.'

Rose popped the last of her sandwich into her mouth, pleased with herself. She was sure Owen and Eleri wouldn't refuse an invitation to spend an evening in the pub with Liam, and Hannah had been going on about meeting him since day one. This way she could kill two birds with one stone.

Liam cleared his throat.

'What does the pub quiz have to do with our current predicament?'

'Ah, yes, I should have explained. It was Hannah who first told me there was bad feeling about you and your business. It was Owen who mentioned that his boss doesn't have a good word to say about your chalet. I thought we could gently quiz them for more details.'

Liam nodded slowly. 'That could work.'

Rose beamed. Liam smiled back at her warily.

'Sorry,' she said, suddenly ashamed. 'I haven't asked how you're feeling. I should have asked straight away instead of crying all over you. And it should have been me getting the food and drinks,' she added. She held the mug of hot chocolate in her two hands and felt the warmth seep into her cold fingers.

'I feel...' he looked down at the contents of his mug. 'I feel pretty awful.' He half-laughed and Rose reached out and lightly touched the sleeve of his jumper.

'I'm sorry I made it worse by running away.'

'You didn't.' He smiled sadly. 'I wanted to know you were OK but I also wanted a reason to get away from the house. I couldn't bear everyone's silent misery.'

'We're going to have to face them again soon,' said Rose.

'Yeah, but I want to enjoy this hot chocolate first — and maybe one of those muffins.' He glanced back at the counter where Rose could just make out the selection of cakes behind a glass cabinet.

'Let me get them,' said Rose, standing quickly.

He made no effort to stop her. 'Thanks — I fancy the raspberry and white chocolate.'

'That sounds good, I think I'll get the salted caramel; it looks particularly gooey.'

She joined the end of the queue and looked back at Liam who was resting his head in one hand and watching the fire.

When she'd thought that Liam and his friends were against her, the world had seemed like a dark and friendless place. She'd only had that feeling for a couple of hours. Liam was living with it daily. It was amazing that he was continuing to laugh and smile and to make sure other people had a good time. Today, he had thought about her and had tried to make her feel better, even though the fact that his business was under attack must be constantly playing around in the back of his mind.

From now on she would not think of herself, even if it did seem as if some-one was out to frame her. She would put all her energy into finding out who was behind the campaign to destroy the suc-cess of Liam's chalet. He deserved her unwavering support and she wouldn't let him down again.

16

It had only taken a couple of phone calls to arrange the pub quiz. Owen and Eleri had been delighted at the prospect of spending the evening with Liam, and Hannah couldn't agree fast enough. They only needed one other person to complete the team and Hannah had said she would sort that out.

Bryn and his family had been more than content to eat a little earlier than normal. When Liam was thankfully out of earshot Bryn had talked about how much a couple needed a date night every now and again. Rose had blushed, but hadn't corrected his assumption that they were together. It served her purposes to let him think that, at least for the evening.

She'd stacked the dishwasher with their plates from dinner and then taken herself off to get ready. Rummaging around in her wardrobe, she tried to find something Liam hadn't seen her in at least a hundred times already. She settled on a pale-blue sleeveless top which she'd worn on New Year's Eve. He'd only seen it on her briefly before she went out with friends and she'd noticed the gleam of appreciation in his eyes before she'd left. She applied a little make-up, taking time to make sure it didn't look as if she'd taken any time at all. Liam had seen her at her absolute worst, whether she was upside down on the side of a mountain or sobbing into his shoulder, but she had her pride — and if they were about to go out together she wanted to look her best.

Not that this was a date, far from it. They were hoping for some information about Owen's employer, something that might help to clear up the mystery. She pushed down a bubble of unease for using her friends like this, but it was for the greater good and her friends wouldn't be any worse off for it. Besides, if she and Liam were subtle her friends need never know they were being interrogated.

Liam was waiting for her in the kitchen wearing a dark blue checked shirt and jeans, hands shoved deep into his pockets. She didn't miss the flicker of appreciation as he took in her outfit.

'You look good,' she said. She was amused to see the tips of his ears turn red.

'You stole my line,' he said, the corner of his lips twitching.

She felt her own skin heat.

'Shall we go?' she croaked.

'Yeah, we should,' although the look in his eyes suggested he'd rather be doing something else. 'Have you got something warmer than that?' he asked.

'Oh, yes, I forgot my coat.' She cringed as she made her way back to her room. She may fancy Liam but it was no reason to act like an idiot in front of him. They'd spent enough time together for her to be relaxed in his company. She pulled a jacket on and headed back to the front door.

Liam had been joined by Bryn and for a moment the two of them continued to discuss tomorrow's skiing conditions. From what Rose could work out they were going to be ideal for skiing over to the next valley. Rose still hadn't made it that far after the abortive weekend when the skis were destroyed, and they'd been so busy since then that there hadn't been the time.

'Well,' said Bryn in his deep, booming voice, 'I'll leave you young lovebirds to have a good evening. Goodnight.' He winked at Rose before slapping Liam good-naturedly on the shoulder and wandering off.

Liam stood by the door as if frozen.

Rose couldn't help but giggle.

'Come on, let's go before he thinks of something else he wants to discuss with you.'

She pulled open the door and stepped into the frosty evening. She heard Liam follow her and close the door behind him.

She turned to look up at the brilliantly clear sky, 'Wow, it's beautiful up here away from the bright lights of a city. Look how many stars you can see.' She gazed up at the twinkling lights hoping Liam would follow her lead with the change of conversation. She didn't want to address the lovebirds comment while they were both still embarrassed about it.

She heard him fall into step beside her.

'I know what you mean. When I first started living at the top of a mountain I bought a guide to the stars so that I could identify the constellations.'

'What can you see tonight?' she asked.

'There's Orion,' he said pointing to the familiar pattern of the famous archer.

'I'm not impressed yet, everyone knows that one,' she teased.

'OK then.' He stopped and looked around for a moment. 'Can you see that cluster of stars? Those are the Pleiades.'

She stopped walking. 'Where?'

He leaned closer to her and she caught the faint smell of his aftershave. 'Sometimes if you look at them directly you can't see them.' He turned her slightly. 'Now can you see them?'

'Oh yes, I do see them. They look like a sort of hazy blob.'

She felt him laugh. 'Yeah, that's the scientific name for them, 'a hazy blob'. I can't understand why you don't have a job at NASA.'

'OK, Mr Clever-clogs, what are they?'

'They're a cluster of stars to the right of Taurus's head and they're one of the youngest clusters we can see. They probably weren't around at the time of the dinosaurs. Now are you impressed?'

'Slightly more than I was earlier.'

He nudged her gently and she laughed.

'OK, I'm impressed. Tell me more.'

They walked slowly to the pub, Liam pointing out constellations as they went, the snow crunching underfoot the only other noise she could hear.

'You were lying when you said sport was your only subject,' said Rose as they got closer to the pub. 'Let's hope they have a section on space.'

'Only if it's on constellations. I don't know anything else about space. I didn't really listen during science lessons. I was too busy thinking about skiing.'

Rose laughed. 'Did you always want to be a professional skier?'

'Yes. My parents are big fans and took us on skiing holidays from the moment we were born, literally in the case of my brother who was only four weeks old on his first trip. Those of us who were too young to ski played in chalets until we were old enough to go out on the slopes. I don't remember a time when I couldn't ski. Mum reckons I could do it before I could walk. They were keen for me to go into the family business, selling cars like my brother and sisters, but they could see my heart wasn't in it. All I've ever wanted to do is ski.'

Rose gazed wistfully up at the stars.

'It must be good to have a definite plan in life.'

'Did you have one . . . ' He seemed to falter before carrying on, 'Well, did you have one before your father died and you started looking after your brothers?'

She tilted her head to one side. 'I have a vague recollection of wanting to be a TV chef but I can't remember when that was. It may have been after he died because that's when I started cooking.'

Liam nodded, 'You could easily be a chef. Do you want to train to be one?'

Rose stopped just outside the pub door.

'I don't think so. I love home cooking but the thought of being in a bustling kitchen environment fills me with fear. See what I mean? I don't have a plan and that scares me a little.'

'Maybe when you've been to many more countries you'll have an idea. Or maybe it's just as good not to have one. Then you get to see more of the world,' said Liam softly.

'Maybe,' she agreed, although she was beginning to think that all she really wanted to do was spend time with Liam — and that wasn't really a career choice.

Liam pulled open the pub door and gestured for her to go in before him.

The air was warm inside with the distinct smell of beer and home cooking. English voices filled the air and Rose spotted Hannah waving at her from the other side of the room. She groaned before she could help herself.

'What's wrong?' asked Liam, as they wended their through the crowds.

She turned back to talk to him. 'Hannah's been trying to set me up on a date with her friend, Ed, and it looks like she's brought him along tonight as the person to make up the numbers.'

She was gratified to feel Liam tense up next to her. Not that he had anything to be jealous about but still, it was good to know he wasn't relaxed by Ed's presence.

'Hi,' she said as they arrived at the table, 'Sorry we're a little late.'

The normally talkative group lapsed into silence with Hannah openly gawping at Liam. Rose hadn't thought that the group would be so star-struck by his presence. She quickly introduced everyone, keeping her voice light and cheerful, hoping that everyone would relax soon. It was going to be a long evening if she was the only one speaking.

'Hi everyone,' said Liam, his natural, relaxed persona returning. 'I'm about to get Rose and me a drink, can I get anyone anything?'

They shook their heads and Hannah mumbled an almost inaudible, 'We've got some, thanks.'

'OK,' Liam said. 'What would you like, Rose?'

'I'll come with you to the bar,' she said, wanting to apologise for her friend's reactions in private. 'I'll have a look at what they've got.'

'I'm sorry,' she said as soon as they were out of earshot. 'I don't know what happened then.'

He chuckled quietly. 'Don't worry about it. That has happened to me before, but not for a while. Not long after I won my first Olympic gold people would either stop me in the street to take a photo or they'd look at me and not be able to say anything at first. By the time we get back to the table they'll have got over it.'

'I hope so. It's not going to be easy to

ask them questions if they've gone mute,' she joked.

The quiz papers had arrived by the time they got back to the table and everyone visibly relaxed as Liam asked them about their specialist pub quiz subject. By the time the quiz started they'd worked out they covered nearly every topic apart from literature. Typically, the first question was about a Shakespeare play. Owen and Liam got into a friendly debate about whether the ship-wrecked twins appeared in *Twelfth Night* or *A Midsummer's Night's Dream*, which lasted for the first half of the quiz. Rose watched her friends visibly relax as Liam acted like everyone else.

'I keep thinking I can look up the answer on my phone,' confessed Liam when they were going over their answers during the half-time break.

'You can't do that,' said Rose scandalised. 'We'd get chucked out.'

'I know, I know ... ' Liam laughed 'Who would like another drink?'

This time everyone accepted a drink

from Liam although Rose made a note to pay him back for half of it when they got home. She knew how strapped for cash he was, but didn't want to embarrass him in front of everyone. Owen and Ed went to help him at the bar while Eleri went to the ladies, saying that was all she seemed to be doing now the baby was getting bigger.

'Should she really be on the slopes?' asked Rose as she watched Eleri disappear in the direction of the toilets. 'She's starting to show.'

'She's not skiing any more,' said Hannah. 'Look, before the boys come back I just want to say I'm sorry for bringing Ed. I thought that if you spent some time with him you'd see what a lovely guy he is, but I can see that's pointless now. You didn't tell me about you and Liam,' Hannah added, her face breaking into a wide grin.

Rose felt heat rush across her face.

'There isn't a me and Liam.'

Hannah hooted with laughter, 'Pull the other one. I may be a bit slow on the uptake but now I've seen you together it's so obvious. You fancy each other something rotten!'

'Shush!' whispered Rose. 'He might hear you.'

'As if that matters. He'd have to be blind not to notice how you feel about him. It's written all over your face.'

Rose touched her face. Her skin was burning. 'Please stop talking about this,' she begged. 'I don't want to be the colour of a beetroot when everyone returns.'

'OK, I'm sorry,' said Hannah but she didn't look contrite. She was grinning as the others headed back from the bar.

'We settled on *Twelfth Night*,' said Liam as he put the drinks down on the table. 'Is everything all right, Rose? You've gone a funny colour.'

Hannah sniggered and Rose nudged her under the table. 'I'm fine. It's a bit hot in here, isn't it?'

Liam glanced at her short sleeves before nodding politely.

'You'll never guess who I've just seen,' said Eleri, returning and sliding in next to Owen.

'Who?' asked Hannah.

'Our horrible boss, Robert Turner, that's who. I don't know why he's turned up tonight. I was looking forward to not spending any time with him,' Eleri pulled a face and took a long sip of her orange juice.

Rose's heart quickened and she looked across at Liam, who was concentrating on his pint, but she could tell from the whites of his knuckles that he was tense.

'Maybe he's come to get a look at you,' Owen said to Liam.

'Hmm?' said Liam, looking up from his pint and smiling vaguely at Owen.

'He overheard us talking about tonight, but I didn't think he'd do anything as weird as coming to the pub himself,' said Eleri, twisting in her seat and looking over in the direction of the toilets.

'Which one is he?' asked Rose, who was sitting opposite Eleri and could see the toilets without having to turn round.

'He's the guy in the red coat,' said Eleri.

Rose pretended to look around the pub for something and let her gaze pass over Robert Turner. He wasn't looking in their direction, but one member of his group stared fixedly at Liam.

For the first time Rose was worried about Liam's safety. It had been her idea to come tonight but she hadn't expected to meet Robert and his cronies. Suddenly the whole thing took on a sinister cast, and she wished she could sneak Liam out and away from potential danger.

The second half of the quiz started but Rose couldn't concentrate on the words. She alternated between staring at her drink and watching Robert.

'Hey,' said Liam, gently nudging her with his knee, 'I thought you said music was your subject so what's the answer?'

'Sorry, I didn't hear the question.'

'The last number one of the Seventies?'

'I wasn't alive then but I think I've heard this question before. Um ... I think it's something about bricks and walls.'

'I know it,' said Owen, scribbling down an answer. 'Well done, Rose.'

'Relax,' whispered Liam under the cover of the next question. 'Nothing's going to happen in front of all these people.'

'But we still have to walk home,' she muttered anxiously.

'I won't let anything happen to you,' said Liam, his breath brushing her cheek.

'It's not me I'm worried about.' She turned and looked at him. Their shoulders were just touching and she could see flecks of yellow in his otherwise blue irises. He smiled softly and she felt her insides melt. He really did have the most delicious smile.

'We'll walk further into the town with the others and get a taxi from the centre,' he said, lightly brushing her fingers under the table.

She nodded but it didn't stop her heart thundering every time she saw Robert move.

'I think we've done well this time,' said Hannah as the quiz came to a close. 'We may not have won but I don't think we'll be at the bottom like last week. Liam should come with us every time.'

'Liam Woods doesn't know the meaning of the word losing, do you, mate?' boomed a loud voice from behind Rose.

Rose didn't need to turn around to know that Robert Turner was behind them. Her knees started to tremble.

'I'm sorry, I don't think we've met,' said Liam politely as he turned to look at the newcomer.

'I'm Robert Turner,' said the man.

Up close Rose could see his large bushy eyebrows in his thick-set face. His teeth were bared in what was probably meant to be a smile. He held out a hand for Liam to shake.

Rose tensed as Liam took the man's hand expecting some sort of aggressive manoeuvre but Robert released his grip after a few seconds.

For a few long awkward moments no one said anything. Rose scrabbled around for something to say that might break the tension. The only thing she could think of to say was to ask if Robert was responsible for the damage in Liam's locker room. That wasn't going to relax anyone!

She looked wildly at Owen who finally seemed to take the hint.

'I didn't expect to see you here tonight, boss.'

Robert frowned. 'I fancied a drink with some of the other landlords. Come over and let me introduce you, Liam. Us chalet owners have to stick together.'

Rose wanted to grab hold of Liam and pin him to the seat but he was a grown man and there was nothing she could do to stop him.

'Of course,' said Liam, smiling calmly. 'It would be good to compare notes with people who have been doing this a lot longer than me. Any tips would be gratefully appreciated.'

Rose noticed the way Robert puffed up with importance.

Liam slipped past her and stood. 'I'll be back in a minute,' he said to her, 'and then we'll head off. I've got an early start in the morning.'

All Rose could do was nod as she watched him cross the pub, Robert Turner hot on his heels.

Owen groaned, 'I'm so sorry, Rose. Your man is in for a very dull few minutes.'

'I hope so,' muttered Rose. 'Does anyone want another drink?'

'I wouldn't mind a hot chocolate,' said Hannah.

'Good idea,' said Rose. 'Shall I get one for everyone?'

There was a chorus of agreement apart from Ed, who downed the rest of his pint and then said he must be off. A twinge of guilt hit Rose's stomach, as she'd pretty much ignored Ed all evening, but then she hadn't asked him to come and she had made it clear to Hannah that she wasn't interested.

She made her way over to the bar, checking in her handbag that she'd brought her phone with her. If anything went wrong she could film it and show it to the police, provided that Liam wasn't in any physical danger. From her position she could just make out Liam and the group of men.

Robert was talking and waving his arms around in a grand gesture. Liam was nodding every so often but didn't appear to be saying anything in response. He looked politely interested and not at all worried.

After several minutes had passed and nothing untoward had happened Rose started to relax. This might be their golden opportunity. If Robert kept talking, he might give something away. She ordered the hot chocolates and staggered back to the table with the weight of the tray.

'Oh, sorry,' said Hannah, taking the trayas she got close to the table. 'I should have come and helped you. I'm getting it all wrong this evening.'

'I'm sorry I ignored Ed,' said Rose as she handed out the drinks.

'You don't need to apologise. You told me again and again you weren't interested. I should have listened.'

Owen looked up at them in surprise. 'I thought you and Liam were together,' he said to Rose.

Rose laughed, 'No. We're not a couple.'

'Well, you act like you are,' said Owen bluntly.

'Ignore him,' said Eleri fondly. 'He has as much tact as a bus. Thanks for introducing us. He seems like a top bloke and I can't wait for next season to try out those improvements he suggested.'

'But . . . ' Owen protested.

'But nothing,' said Eleri. 'Now stop talking, he's coming back over and we don't want to embarrass Rose. Besides we owe him an apology. If we hadn't opened our big mouths earlier Liam wouldn't have spent the last ten minutes being bored to tears by our boss.'

There wasn't time to quiz Liam when he got back to the table as the compère announced he was going to go through the answers. Liam smiled at Rose in answer to her questioning frown and shook his head. Frustratingly she couldn't tell what he meant by that.

It seemed to Rose as if the compère took an inordinately long time to read through the answers this evening. Normally she enjoyed the banter between him and the crowd but tonight she willed everyone to stop talking and get on with it. Her silent entreaties didn't work, and time passed slowly. Eventually all the papers were marked and they were handed back their own sheet.

Hannah looked through the marked paper quickly. 'We've done really well,' she squealed excitedly. 'Imagine if we won!'

In the end they came second, which meant they walked away with a bottle of cheap white wine to share between the six of them.

'You have it,' said Rose to Hannah as they pulled on their coats.

'Are you sure?' asked Hannah, clutching the prize with glee.

'I'm sure,' said Rose, who would have said anything to get everyone to hurry up.

'It's not really the prize but the glory of

coming second,' said Hannah, grinning. 'I bet I'm feeling as fabulous as you did when you won those gold medals, Liam.'

Liam laughed. 'I think you're feeling even better than that.'

'Yeah, probably. I mean anyone can go down a mountain on skis but it takes real brain power to come second in a pub quiz!'

Everyone laughed at Hannah's evident delight, even Rose, who dearly wished her friend would put on her coat like the rest of them and let them all leave.

Finally they waved goodbye to the others, after plenty of hugs and back-slapping congratulations, and set off back up towards the chalet.

'Well?' said Rose the instant they were out of earshot.

'I don't think it's him.'

'What? You must be wrong. It's got to be him.'

'He was pompous and a real know-it-all but I don't think he's got it in him to trash my hotel. He just didn't seem the type.'

'Tell me the conversation from the start,' Rose demanded.

Liam grinned. 'Yes, boss.' He gave her a mock salute. 'He introduced me to his colleagues, making a bit of a meal of what a great skier I am, which of course we know is the truth.' Liam laughed at his own joke.

'Get on with it,' Rose complained, waving her hands around to try and hurry him along.

'Then he proceeded to tell me how great his own chalet was and to let me know all the things he thought I was probably doing wrong. I nodded and pretended that all he said was wise and wonderful and we parted as great friends. And, before you ask, I didn't interrogate him about his movements last weekend but I bet we could find that out from Owen and Eleri.'

Rose stopped walking.

'But if it's not him, then who is it?'

Liam stopped as well. 'I don't know.'

'Could it be more than one person?'

Liam pulled a face. 'I hope not. I'd

like to think I'm not so universally disliked that more than one person is trying to destroy my business.'

Rose started walking again and Liam fell into step beside her.

'The stopcock and trashing the locker room has to have been done by someone nearby, but the other stuff could have been done by someone remotely. I mean someone in Australia could have written the website reviews.'

'I don't know anyone in Australia,' he said, raising an eyebrow.

'You know what I mean.'

'Listen, Rose,' said Liam, coming to a halt just before the entrance, Rose stopped in front of him. There was barely any space between them, Liam didn't move away. Rose's heart began to beat faster.

'I wanted to talk to you about what Bryn said. You see, the thing is … '

Deep in Liam's jacket his phone rang, loud in the still night air. Liam jumped and stepped a little away from her, breaking the moment. He reached into his pocket and fished it out.

'It's Gareth. I'm sorry, I'm going to have to take this in case it's something to do with the insurance. Can we talk about this tomorrow?'

'Of course,' said Rose, smiling up at him.

He smiled back before answering the phone and pushing open the front door, allowing Rose to step in before him.

He strode off into the house, leaving Rose by the front door, her knees wobbling slightly. Whatever Liam had been about to say, it had nothing to do with vandalism and everything to do with them.

She slipped out of her jacket and folded it over her arm. She wandered slowly to her bedroom in case the call to Gareth was over quickly, but by the time she was pulling on her pyjamas she could still hear his voice rumbling from his bedroom. She didn't know the details but Liam had hinted that his insurance company weren't being very forthcoming. He was having to jump through hoops and provide copious details.

Luckily his friends had more than one set of skis and none of them had brought the equipment they raced with, but it was still a blow, and the worry had etched further lines around Liam's eyes.

Curled up in her bed, sleep took a long time to come. Every time she closed her eyes she saw Liam's face as he'd stood outside the house, the look in his eyes unreadable.

Her instinct cried out that he'd been about to confess to having feelings for her — but he could just have easily been about to let her down gently. If only Gareth hadn't phoned right at that moment!

17

Bryn was already munching a croissant when Rose entered the dining room next morning.

'Hello,' she said. 'I was just coming to see whether anyone was ready for their cooked breakfast this morning. Would you like yours now, or do you want to wait for the others?'

'The others won't be long so I'll wait. Why don't you join me for a cuppa before they get here?'

Rose was torn — she didn't want to be rude to Bryn, who not only was a guest but also one of her favourites so far, but she also had a lot to do this morning.

'Thank you,' she said, perching on the edge of a dining seat. 'I'll have a quick one.'

Bryn loved to talk and it was some time before Rose was able to extract herself to go and cook breakfast, only managing to make her move when Bryn's wife Ann arrived and lovingly told her husband to let Rose go.

'Will you come with us today, Rose?' Bryn asked as she moved away from the table.

'Oh, no. I've got to tidy up and cook dinner.'

'We don't mind eating later — or, how about this Ann? Why don't we take Rose and Liam out to dinner to thank them for two fabulous weeks at this lovely chalet?'

'What a lovely idea, Bryn,' said Ann, smiling sweetly. 'Please do say you'll both come. I'd like to treat you after you've been so good to us.'

Rose stammered her thanks and said she'd best check with Liam.

She found him in the kitchen laying rashers of bacon on the grill.

'You don't need to do that,' she said, trying to take the bacon from him.

'Don't be silly. If you're entertaining the guests then I'll make the breakfast. They're just as happy talking to you as to me.'

He carried on seeing to the bacon so she opened the packet of sausages and dumped them into a frying pan.

'Bryn wants us to go out to dinner with him and Ann this evening, and for me to come skiing with you all today.'

She waited for Liam to protest but all he said was, 'That's a good idea. You never did get to see the next valley, which is where we're planning to visit today. It's a good opportunity for you to see it because I'm not sure when we'll have the time again.'

'But they can't buy us dinner when they've paid for us to feed them,' she protested, turning the sausages over.

'Don't forget they got a huge discount for this week. If that's what they want to do then I say we go for it. It will be good not to have to wash up this evening.' He grinned at her as he slipped the bacon under the heat.

'I'll still have to tidy,' said Rose, thinking of the bathroom that would need cleaning before the guests got back for their afternoon shower.

'How about you ski over to the next valley with us and then come back a little earlier on your own? Will that give you enough time to do everything?'

Liam opened the fridge and pulled out two large bottles of freshly squeezed orange juice.

'Yes,' said Rose, jiggling the sausages, which were beginning to turn brown. 'I'd love a day skiing. It just sounds too good to be true.'

'I'll help you with the tidying when I get back,' said Liam, loading a tray with various drinks.

She smiled at him; he really was the best boss. She was so glad she'd got a job with him rather than with someone like Robert Turner — and that wasn't just because she found him so desperately attractive.

'If we're going to be out all day then there won't be much to do,' she conceded.

'Great. I'll take this through and let Bryn know we're going to take him up on his generous offer. Let's hope he isn't thinking of taking us to a fast food restaurant!' Liam winked and took the tray.

She hadn't seen much of Liam this morning but there had been enough time to finish off last night's conversation if he'd really wanted to. Maybe something Gareth had said last night had changed his mind. She got the impression Gareth wasn't too keen on her. Although he'd apologised profusely for upsetting her when she'd last seen him, the way he'd looked at her suggested he didn't quite trust her.

Rose pulled the bacon out from under the heat and used tongs to turn it over. Before coming out here, her life had been not dull but safe and contented. Now everything was up in the air and Rose felt as if she was living on the edge of her nerves. It was exhilarating!

'Should I make a packed lunch for everyone if we're going to be out all day?' she asked Liam when he came back into the kitchen.

'No, I've an arrangement with a cafe

in the next valley. It's all part of the cost of the holiday. I'll ring and book you in too. Also, the restaurant Bryn wants to take us to tonight is sufficiently swanky so we don't have to worry about limp burgers and cardboard fries.'

'Excellent,' said Rose, pulling the bacon out of the grill. 'I think this is done. Do you want some?'

'Yes please, and Bryn would like it if you made yourself up a plate too, and came and joined us.'

Rose wanted to ask Liam what she should say if Bryn made any more comments about them being a couple but she lost her nerve and meekly took a portion for herself without saying anything.

She was saved any embarrassment on the lovebird front because Bryn was thrilled she was going to join them on their skiing trip and, when he found out they were going down routes she'd never seen before, he wasted no time in telling her how much she was going to enjoy herself.

Rose's stomach twinged when she

realised this week was probably the last time she'd spend time with Bryn and his wife. Even if they came back to Liam's chalet next year, she would have moved on and he'd have a different assistant helping him. She might be in Thailand or somewhere exotic.

Her heart gave a disappointed thump as she thought about life without Liam's smiles and thoughtfulness. But now she had considered not being here for the season next year, it was impossible not to think about the implications of that and to come to the logical conclusion: there was no future for her and Liam as a couple.

She carried the plates through to the kitchen and began loading them into the dishwasher. Tears pricked her eyes even as she told herself not to be silly. Liam was lovely but he was born to be on the mountain, whereas she still hadn't found her forever place.

He wanted to be here, and he knew that she wanted to see more of the world. She resolved to let him down gently in the remote possibility that he did confess to having feelings for her. It was the right thing to do — but just thinking about leaving him made her wretched with distress.

'Are you all right?' asked Liam, striding into the kitchen a few minutes later. 'You don't have the face of someone looking forward to a day of glorious skiing. Is the thought of not cleaning those bathrooms upsetting you that much?'

She laughed, despite her gloomy thoughts.

'No, I'm looking forward to the skiing. I'll go and get changed and meet you downstairs.'

She felt a tear trickle down her face as she pulled on the ski jacket he'd bought for her and she shook her head crossly. She was making herself miserable for no reason at all. For all she knew, he'd been about to discuss the week's menu with her last night and not confess to undying devotion. She would enjoy the next seven weeks with him and not look back when she left.

That was, provided they found out who was behind the attacks on Liam. If they didn't, the fact that someone was out there trying to hurt Liam would haunt her wherever she was in the world.

* * *

The sun blazed down on them from a bright blue, cloudless sky as they meandered down to the start of the bubble lift. Today Rose didn't mind being squashed onto it because it meant she was pressed right up against Liam, who shifted slightly so his arm was curved around her.

'Do you remember that strange phone call you had when we first came?' asked Bryn as the lift juddered up the mountain. 'Did you ever find who was behind it? Have you had any other mishaps?'

Liam glanced at Rose and then told Bryn the whole story, starting from the initial problems he had before he'd bought the site right up until the break-in last week.

'It sounds as if it must be someone who knows you well,' Bryn said as they sailed over tree tops.

'I think so too,' said Rose.

'I can't think of anyone who hates me,' said Liam for the hundredth time.

'I can't imagine people disliking you either,' said Bryn. 'But someone obviously does. Maybe an ex-girlfriend because you hooked up with Rose?'

Beside her Liam stiffened. Rose hid her grin by looking down at the floor.

'Rose and I aren't a couple,' said Liam rather awkwardly.

Bryn only snorted with laughter.

After Liam's denial Rose half expected him to move his arm away but he kept it where it was. Gradually she relaxed and leaned into him as the conversation moved on.

She couldn't get Bryn's comment about someone close to Liam being responsible for all his problems out of her mind. That left Sarah as the front runner in the very short list of suspects. She'd looked very convincing when she was snuggling up to Paul, but was that all an act? She'd been very quick to agree with Gareth that Rose could be responsible for the damaged skis, which could have been an attempt to throw the suspicion away from herself.

Or could it be someone even closer to home? Liam had told her his parents were keen for him to be part of the family business. It was just possible they had set things in motion to try and stop Liam's business being a success. But then they weren't over here and couldn't have tinkered with the pipes, let alone broken all that equipment. Liam appeared to be very close to his family so really it was unlikely to be them.

Even so, she was still trying to work out whether it was feasible for his mum and dad to pay someone to sabotage Liam's business when the lift arrived at the top of the mountain.

Liam led the mall over to the start of the run and talked them through the twists and turns. He was so animated and clear and her heart squeezed with pride as she watched how the others were focused intently on his words.

The morning passed quickly. The loveliness of the valley hadn't been exaggerated and the slopes were wide and relatively free from people. Rose's legs were pleasantly exhausted when they stopped for lunch.

'Shall we sit outside?' asked Bryn. 'I know there's all this snow around, but I'm boiling.'

Rose was only too happy to rid herself of her ski jacket and to flop onto one of the wooden benches outside.

'I never expected to get a tan while I was out here,' she said, turning her face to the sun.

'I got burned on my first skiing trip but unfortunately I was wearing my goggles at the time so I had a horrible tan line,' laughed Bryn, using his finger to outline where his goggles had left pale skin behind.

Over a lunch of thick chicken and vegetable soup, Bryn and Liam discussed the best places to ski that afternoon. Rose looked at the map once they'd picked out a route.

'I think I'll head back after lunch,' she said and smiled when everyone protested.

'Thank you, but I'm not as good at skiing as the rest of you and my legs are tired.'

'Then you must promise me you will go home and have a bath,' said Bryn's wife. 'I don't want to come back to a spotless bathroom.'

Rose laughed, 'In that case I will certainly spend the afternoon indulging myself, thank you.'

'You should try the hot tub,' suggested Liam with a wink.

Rose flushed as she imagined spending the afternoon in the hot tub with Liam. She'd never seen him without at least a jumper on, but she imagined he'd have a deliciously toned chest from all the exercise he did.

She said her goodbyes after they'd all enjoyed some zabaglione and the others headed deeper into the valley. She slowly made her way to a bank of lifts and got on one to take her back to the top of the mountain. From there she skied slowly back to the chalet, taking the time to enjoy the magnificent scenery on the route.

* * *

Back at the chalet she slipped her skis back into her locker and then made sure everything was securely locked up. Liam wasn't taking any chances and had installed CCTV, as well as a thicker padlock and stronger door. When she was satisfied no one was getting in while she soaked in the bath, she made her way upstairs.

Knowing she wouldn't be able to enjoy her afternoon if she hadn't at least checked the guests' bathrooms, she went to take a look. Once she'd topped up various toiletries and given everything a basic wipe down, she went to run the water. She rang her mum while she was waiting for the bath to fill.

'Hello, love,' said her mum. 'How are things?'

'Everything's fantastic,' said Rose, relaxing as steam filled the room and the warmth began to seep into her skin.

'There's not been anymore unpleasantness?'

'Not since the last time we spoke,' said Rose, slipping out of her salopettes and dumping them on the bedroom floor.

'Are the police any nearer to catching who did it?' her mother pressed.

'I don't think they're trying, Mum,' said Rose as she climbed into the bath and let the warm water envelop her.

'Do you still think it's that local landlord? I've forgotten his name.'

'Robert. I don't know. Liam seems to think he's a buffoon but otherwise he's harmless. To me it seems more likely to be Liam's ex-girlfriend.'

'Ah, well, nothing more may come of it. There are only seven weeks left, aren't there?'

'That's right. I've booked my flight home. I can't wait to see you all.'

'Have you decided where you're going next?'

'I've spent some time looking recently. I've always wanted to go to Spain, so I might go there. I haven't decided yet.'

They chatted until the water began to cool and Rose climbed out, wrapping a large fluffy towel around her.

'I'm going to go now, Mum. I need to get ready for tonight.'

'Are you going anywhere special?'

'I'm being taken to a swanky restaurant.'

'By Liam?'

'By one of the guests.'

'Is he handsome?'

Rose laughed. 'He's very dapper but he's married and old enough to be my dad. He's taking us all, so it's not a romantic trip.'

'That's disappointing. But now that Liam and his girlfriend aren't getting back together there's nothing stopping you having a holiday romance.'

'I'm going to be leaving in seven weeks so I don't think that's a good idea,' she said.

'Rose, don't take everything so seriously. Just because your father and I were childhood sweethearts it doesn't mean that every boyfriend you have has to be potential husband material. You can date someone just for the fun of it.'

'Mum! I am scandalised!'

'Oh, Rose, don't be naughty. I'm not suggesting anything rude.'

But Rose was giggling too much to respond to her mum.

'I'm going to go now,' said her mum with laughter in her voice.

'Bye, Mum. Love you.'

'Love you too, even if you do have a dirty mind!'

Rose chuckled and switched off the phone.

She couldn't imagine suggesting to Liam that they have a passionate short-lived fling! She imagined the tips of his ears going bright red and him shuffling on his feet as he did whenever he was embarrassed. She giggled to herself again.

She pulled on skinny jeans and went back to her wardrobe to see if a new top had miraculously appeared while she was out. It hadn't. She could probably ring Hannah and borrow something. They were about the same shape, although Hannah was a lot taller.

For now she pulled on a jumper and felt her stomach rumble. She glanced at the clock. It was still ages until dinner, so it was obviously time for cake. A large chunk of Victoria sponge wouldn't spoil her appetite for a meal out.

She'd made the cake yesterday and only half of it was left. Really she should make another one, but the combination of the long ski followed by an indulgent soak in the bath had left her boneless. The thought of standing up in the kitchen for the length of time it took to whip up some batter didn't fill her with enthusiasm.

She took her slice of cake and a mug of tea into the staff sitting room and settled into the comfy armchair she'd begun to think of as hers.

She was licking her fingertip to better scoop up the crumbs when she heard the front door open and close.

She sat up straight in her chair.

Bryn and Ann were out with Liam. They were all skiing. To get into the house, they would have to go via the locker room. No one should be coming through the front door.

Quietly she put her plate down on the footstool in front of her. She crept to the sitting room door and listened carefully.

Nothing moved.

She straightened from her slightly hunched position; perhaps she had imagined it. But no, there was the sound of someone moving again.

She was no longer alone in the house.

18

Rose crept across the kitchen careful to avoid bumping into the chairs, which would scrape against the tiled kitchen floor if touched.

Fortunately she'd left the door to the main body of the house open and she slipped through it quickly. Once she was on the other side, she stood listening carefully.

Guests tended to go straight up to their room when they'd finished skiing for the day. Once out of their thick skiwear, they often ran the bath or got changed into their swimming costumes to take advantage of the pool or hot tub. Either that or they came to the kitchen looking for food or drinks.

She strained her ears listening out for the sound of running water, but silence reigned until she made out a faint clunk from beneath her.

She scooted quickly down the stairs and stepped into the locker room, expecting to find someone pulling off their ski boots. A discarded hat lay on the floor but otherwise the room was empty. Rose picked up the hat and tested the locker room door. It was still firmly locked. She twisted the hat between her fingers and then smoothed it out and placed it on the bench.

A clunk sounded above her. She ran her hands through her hair and debated what to do. She could either head back up to the staff quarters and phone the police, or she could go and see whether there really was someone upstairs. It was possible her mind was playing tricks on her.

If she phoned the police and the unusual noise turned out to be one of the guests coming home early and deciding to take a swim, she would look foolish and could get into trouble for wasting police time. She'd look even more foolish if it turned out the noise she'd heard was the wind banging an open window.

Softly she climbed the stairs. She peered into the games room first. It was empty.

She heard a clunk again, louder this time, and she turned to look into the swimming pool. The water shimmered invitingly in the late afternoon light. There was no one here. She'd obviously been mistaken. She turned to head back down and heard that mysterious clunk again.

She looked at the pool, convinced that the sound was coming from that direction but the water was still. She moved slowly around the room, her back against the wall.

At the far end of the room she noticed one of sliding doors was ajar. She was sure it hadn't been like that earlier. She took a step towards it and then hesitated. The person responsible for the attacks against Liam was probably out there. Did she really want to confront them by herself?

Then she heard the unmistakable sound of plastic being snapped, and anger swept through her. She stormed towards the sound determined to stop whatever was happening. She pulled open the sliding door fully and stopped in her tracks.

'What are you doing here?' she demanded.

Gareth stood up from his hunched position by the hot tub and turned to her, his red hair glinting in the sunlight.

'Hello, Rose. I didn't realise you were in or I would have come to say hello.'

'What are you doing?' she asked again.

'Liam called me. There's a problem with the hot tub and he wanted me to take a look at it.'

Rose shook her head slowly. 'Liam has someone come out to take a look at the hot tub once a week. He wouldn't ask you to check it.'

For a long moment Gareth stared at her.

Rose put her arms behind her back so he wouldn't see her fingers tremble.

Gareth dropped the spanner he was holding and it hit the terrace with a thud.

'Look, Rose, I don't expect you to understand…'

'No, I really don't. Liam is one of your best friends. Why are you doing this to him? I assume you're the one who's been behind everything?'

Gareth's look was pained. 'Yes, it was me — but I need to explain … '

Rose folded her arms. 'Go on, I'm waiting.'

Gareth sighed. 'Liam is a great skier. I don't expect you to fully understand how good he is. He's far superior to everyone else in our team. He can look at a slope and read it like other people do a book.'

'So far you've not told me anything I don't know already,' said Rose coldly.

'He's still young. He's far too young to retire. He should still be racing. He should still be racing with me.'

'Are you saying that you've tried to sabotage his business because you miss him?'

'Not exactly.' Gareth shifted on his feet. 'Without him on our team our ranking has dropped significantly and that affects our sponsorship deals. We need him to compete with us. You can understand that, surely.'

Rose shook her head.

'You mean, you're doing this for money?'

Gareth sighed. 'No, I'm doing this for the team — and for him. Look, I know this probably seems insane to you, Rose, but you must see how Liam was born to be on the mountain. He doesn't realise it yet but he's made a huge mistake leaving the racing circuit so soon.'

Rose rubbed her temple. How was it that Gareth was making his vindictive vandalism sound as if he was behaving reasonably? She turned to walk away from him. She needed to phone the police and try and get hold of Liam.

'Rose,' said Gareth before she could step towards the sanctuary of the chalet. 'I would appreciate it if you didn't tell Liam about this.'

Rose huffed out a laugh and turned back slightly. 'I have to tell him, Gareth. I'm sorry that it's going to damage your friendship but the way you've behaved over the last few months has devastated him emotionally and financially. He doesn't deserve to be treated like this.'

'He won't believe you,' said Gareth, raising his voice. 'I've been his friend for years; you've only known him five minutes. He'll think you're trying to cause trouble.'

'I'm still going to tell him. He deserves to know. He can make his own mind up whether or not he believes me.'

'I'll pay you!' said Gareth and for the first time Rose could hear the desperation in his voice.

'I don't want your money,' she said slowly.

'Come on, Rose. Everyone has a price.'

'How many other people have you paid?' Rose asked quietly.

Gareth scrunched his face, 'I'll make it worth your while. I gave Gareth's previous assistant a thousand to say she'd broken her foot but I'm asking you to do a lot more, so I'll double it if you want it.'

'You want to pay me two thousand pounds not to say anything to Liam?' Rose clarified.

'I'll throw in another thousand if you want.' He sounded hopeful, he thought he'd got her onside.

She was about to seriously disappoint him.

'Liam has been incredible this season. He's worked long hours, taught me to ski and has taken everything you've thrown at him in his stride. He's never once treated me as a skivvy, and I would never betray him.'

'I'll make it five thousand then.'

'No,' said Rose, stepping towards the chalet.

'Rose, stop!' He grabbed her arm, his fingers biting painfully through her jumper.

'Let go of me!' She tried to inject authority into her voice, but it came out shaky.

'Not until you see reason.'

Rose turned to look at Gareth. His eyes were wild and unfocused. Fear began to prick her heart and she tugged to try and release herself. He held on tighter.

'Let go of her.'

It was the most welcome voice she'd ever heard. 'Liam!' she breathed, her knees weakening at the sight of him.

'Liam,' said Gareth, dropping her arm abruptly. 'I got here earlier and found Rose tampering with the hot tub. I've been trying to reason with her but she's … well quite frankly, I think she has a screw loose. I did warn you.'

Rose gasped and her eyes flew to Liam. His brow was drawn and his lips were thin. He was staring at both of them as if he'd never seen them before. She wanted to yell that it wasn't her, that it was all Gareth, but her words failed her.

'I was standing inside,' said Liam, a quiet rage filling his voice. 'I heard everything.'

Gareth paled even more. 'I can explain!'

'You already did. To Rose. I heard. You want me to return to competitive skiing. I'm sorry to disappoint you, but that's never going to happen. I know I could, but I don't want to, I've moved on to something different.'

'But we need you and you're wasted here. Get someone to run the chalet for you — Rose would do. She's a great cook and you said yourself she's incredibly organised. Your business would be safe in her hands.'

Rose gasped at Gareth's audacity. How could he think Liam would ever work with him again? The trust between them was ruined forever! How could Gareth not see that?

'If you leave now and make no further attempts to sabotage my business I won't press charges,' said Liam coldly.

Gareth rocked back as if he'd been punched.

'Why won't you even consider coming back?' he demanded.

'I am done with professional skiing. Even if my business crumbles down around my ears I won't be coming back, Gareth.'

'You're making a terrible mistake,'

stated Gareth plainly.

'I want you to leave,' Liam repeated.

'Fine!' Gareth snapped. 'But don't expect to come crawling back to me when you realise what you've done.'

Gareth pushed past Rose, knocking her into Liam whose arms automatically came around her and held her up.

'Careful,' Liam growled at Gareth.

Gareth said nothing as he strode away. Seconds later they heard the front door slam shut.

Suddenly, all the strength rushed out of Rose's legs and she collapsed against Liam's chest. He held her tightly and she shook uncontrollably.

'I think he might be insane,' she whispered.

Liam gave a surprised laugh.

'There's no doubt about it. Are you feeling strong enough to move? We should get you back inside before we both freeze to death.'

'Yes, I'm fine,' she said, but she made no move to pull herself out of his arms and he didn't let her go. They shuffled awkwardly into the chalet and Liam closed the sliding doors behind them.

'Do you think he's done permanent damage to the hot tub?' she asked once the warmth of the room began to work its magic.

'I don't know. From here, it looks as if he's pulled the protective case off some of the wiring. I'll take a proper look at it later.'

'I'm so sorry, Liam.'

'Why are you sorry? You've done nothing wrong. In fact you were amazing just now.'

'I know, but he was your friend. It must be a bit of a shock.'

'I don't think I've processed it yet. It'll probably hit me later.'

His arms tightened around her and she rested her head on his chest, enjoying the sensation of the rise and fall of his steady breathing. Tears pricked the back of her eyes and she shuddered.

'Are you OK?' whispered Liam.

'I'm a bit wobbly,' she confessed, although she wasn't sure whether that was because of her encounter with Gareth or because Liam was holding her so close.

He ran his fingers down her back in a comforting gesture, leaving a trail of tingling skin in his wake.

'Thank you for not accepting his money, by the way,' he said after a long moment of silence.

She laughed. 'You never know, I may have accepted if he'd offered more.'

She felt him smile against her hair.

'You wouldn't have. I'm serious though, your loyalty means a lot to me.'

Lightly she pushed against his chest. He loosened his arms enough to look down at her. She waited for him to say something. He opened his mouth as if about to speak but their gaze caught and neither of them moved.

An emotion she couldn't read flickered in his eyes. She held her breath as his mouth slowly moved towards hers.

'Oh! Sorry!' came Bryn's cheerful voice from the doorway across the room. 'I didn't realise you two were in here.'

Liam dropped his arms and Rose reluctantly stepped away from him.

Lovely though Bryn was, him standing there in tight swimming trunks ruined whatever had been about to happen! Besides Bryn thought they were already a couple and wouldn't have realised he was interrupting one of the most monumental moments of Rose's life.

'Did you enjoy the rest of your ski?' she asked Bryn brightly. It wasn't his fault he'd arrived when he had.

'It was fabulous, Rose dear,' said Ann, stepping into the room behind Bryn wearing a tangerine-orange swimming costume.

The two guests lowered themselves into the pool all the while chatting away to Rose about their afternoon. Behind her, Rose felt Liam move away from her. Seconds later, she heard him slip outside towards the damaged hot tub.

She managed to keep her smile fixed in place as she listened to their guests but her heart hurt at the potentially wonderful missed opportunity.

19

Rose fiddled with her hair, trying to get her reflection to look better but it remained stubbornly like her mood — flat.

There was only one week to go until the season ended and, with her flight back to Britain booked as soon as it finished, time had run out for her and Liam.

Over the last few weeks they'd barely had any spare time together. Private moments were interrupted by guests wanting spare towels or more cake or something that took them away from each other, and they'd both worked extra hard to make sure the season ended with Liam securely in profit.

The fallout from Gareth's betrayal had been bigger than either of them had anticipated and Liam was still reeling from the aftermath. For a few weeks she'd hardly seen Liam smile and that had broken her heart. As things returned to normal he'd relaxed again, but the time for them to be together had ended.

Today was their last free Wednesday afternoon. They were going to ski for the whole time and Rose had stopped hoping for anything more than to leave Italy as good friends. They couldn't start a relationship with only a few days left together and she didn't want her heart to get hurt any more than it was likely to be by the simple fact of parting from him forever.

Giving up on her hair, she picked up her ski jacket and made her way into the kitchen. Liam was sitting at the kitchen table hunched over his phone.

'Would you like a cup of tea before we go?' she asked.

He looked up, a frown creasing his forehead.

'No thanks, I'm ready now, if you are.'

He stood and slipped his phone into his pocket.

'Is everything all right?' she asked tentatively.

'I've had another message from Gareth,' he said, his shoulders tense.

'What does he say this time?'

'It's a kind of apology.'

'For what aspect?' she asked incredulously.

Liam huffed out a laugh and shrugged on his jacket. 'For all of it. I think now that our friends are coming down on my side he's realised that he needs to backtrack or he'll be out of the team altogether.'

'I'm amazed he tried to blame it all on you in the first place,' said Rose, following Liam on the familiar route down to the locker room. 'He has an unbelievably huge self-belief. I've never met anyone quite like him.'

Liam had been reluctant to tell their mutual friends what Gareth had done to him, and that kindness had turned out to be a mistake. Gareth had wasted no time in going to Liam's former teammates and trying to twist the situation so that it looked as if Liam was being spiteful and vindictive. It had taken many phone calls and visits to sort out and it had left Liam exhausted and downhearted.

Rose's heart had ached to see him looking so out of sorts and she had thrown herself even harder into looking after the chalet to take the burden off him.

While Gareth hadn't directly ruined a chance of a romance between her and Liam, his actions had certainly meant they had no time to spend together. As far as Rose was concerned, this added to his list of crimes.

'When you say 'a kind of apology', what do you mean?' she asked.

'He's managed to spin it so that somehow it's still all my fault but he wants us to draw a line under everything that happened and start afresh. I guess I can't be on bad terms with him or I'll make life awkward for other people, but I certainly won't be inviting him to stay at my house again.'

'How did you ski with him for so many years and not realise he was totally bonkers?' asked Rose as she pulled her skis out of her locker.

Liam laughed and Rose was relieved to see the light flicker back on in his eyes. Even his shoulders relaxed.

'I guess I'm not very observant. But let's not talk about him any more. I don't want to ruin our last day together on the slopes.' He smiled warmly at her and Rose's heart simultaneously swooped and dived.

She loved his smile, she would bask in it all day if she were allowed to but knowing this was their last ski together was making her miserable. Brushing the feeling aside and vowing to enjoy the day regardless she followed Liam out to the mountainside and clipped on her skis.

'Where would you like to go?' asked Liam when they'd arrived at the lifts.

'I know it's not exciting for a high-octane skier like you but I'd really like to go down the Snake's Head pass. The views are stunning and the slopes are easy so I don't have to fear for my life.'

'I thought you were past that now,' said Liam turning in the direction of the right ski lift.

'I've learned to love skiing but strapping two slim bits of plastic to my feet and hurling myself down a mountain still doesn't feel natural to me.'

He laughed and joined the back of the button lift queue. 'Are you going to stay sitting on this time or am I going to be treated to one of your spectacular falls?'

She laughed with him and Gareth was quickly forgotten as they reminisced about their past skiing season.

* * *

By the time Liam suggested they stop for a break Rose's jaw hurt from grinning so much. The way Liam made her laugh was one of the many things she loved about him.

He pulled over to the side of the mountain and they sat down on the snow, their salopettes keeping them warm and dry.

'I brought hot chocolate,' said Liam, pulling the now familiar flask from his rucksack.

Rose throat was tight with tears as he poured the richly-coloured drink into two small cups. She loved that he'd planned ahead, knowing her well enough to bring her favourite beverage up a mountain just so that they could drink it together.

She swallowed a few times until the blockage in her throat eased and she was able to thank him as he handed her a cup.

They sat in silence for a while, watching skiers whizz down the mountain past them, their brightly coloured bobble hats flashing by in the breeze. Rose couldn't turn to look at Liam; she worried that if she did her feelings would be clearly written across her face.

The thought of returning to Britain without him was twisting her stomach into knots.

'I never did build a snowman,' she said when their silence threatened to overwhelm her.

'What was that?' asked Liam, seeming to come round from a very deep thought.

'My main aim when I came out here

was to build a snowman,' Rose explained. 'I never got a chance to when I was younger because I'd never really seen snow before.'

'Are you serious?' Liam looked at her, his eyebrows raised incredulously.

'Yes, I lived by the coast and the winters were always mild. I've only ever known a few brief flurries. I've never had a snowball fight either.'

'Never … ? Well, we'll have to rectify that. Let's start with a snowman.'

He unclipped his skis and stood them upright in the snow.

'What, now?'

'Yes, now. Come on. We'll make one here and he can stand watch over this amazing view.'

She disengaged her own skis and put them next to his.

Very quickly they rolled together enough snow to make a large stomach.

'What are we going to do for eyes and a nose?' Rose asked as they started on the head.

'One of us will have to come back with

a carrot,' he laughed. 'Or we make one out of snow.'

'Let's make it out of snow,' she said. 'I'll do the nose and eyes. You finish the head. He's a bit wonky,' she said stepping back and looking at the finished product. 'But as it's my first attempt, I love him. Stand next to him so I can take a photo. You may need to squat a little bit so that you're the same height,' she added.

'I think sitting would be better,' said Liam. 'He's a bit stumpy.'

Rose didn't have any photos of Liam so she took several now that she had the chance without it being awkward. She wanted something to remember him by and although she could look up pictures of him on the internet, it wasn't the same as having something personal.

'Let's take a selfie together with him,' said Liam and he patted the snow next to him, inviting her to sit there.

Rose joined him on the ground and held her face next to his so she could get them both in the frame. Even though they weren't quite touching she could sense the warmth of his skin, and she longed to move that extra few millimetres to touch her face against his.

Instead she put her phone back in her pocket and moved away.

'Shall we get going?' she asked, even though she wanted to stay right here on this mountainside with him forever.

'In a moment … Rose, I wanted to ask you something,' said Liam his gaze fixed on a distant mountain peak.

'Yes?' she said a few minutes later when he still hadn't said anything.

He cleared his throat. 'What are your plans for next week?'

'Um … '

He knew what her plans were. Help him tidy up the chalet once the last of the guests had gone home and then get on a plane and head home.

'I mean when you get back to Britain,' he finally clarified.

'Oh, right. I'm going to spend a lot of time with my mum and, if they're not too busy for their older sister, my brothers too.'

Liam nodded, 'I never asked but is there ... ? I mean I kind of got the impression that there wasn't, but... well, is it possible you might be going back to a guy?'

Liam was resolutely not looking at her but Rose watched as colour swept across his cheeks. Her stomach fizzed. 'No, there's no guy back home.'

Liam nodded again. 'So after you've spent time with your family, what are you going to do?'

'Look for another job,' she said quietly. She wished he would turn and look at her. It might be easier to work out where this conversation was going if she could read the expression in his eyes.

'I had an email from Bryn yesterday.'

Rose sat straighter. This wasn't where she was expecting him to go. She'd hoped for a minute there that ... but no. The feelings building up inside her must all be one-sided. She thought he'd been about to open up with a declaration of some sort but instead he wanted to talk about one of their guests.

'What did he have to say?' she asked, trying to inject her voice with enthusiasm.

Liam cleared his throat again. 'His friend is looking for someone to manage a couple of luxury villas he owns in Southern Spain. He thought it might be of interest. It'll be very hot, if that's an incentive.' His eyes quickly cut to her and then away again.

Rose pulled in a shaky breath. Here she was getting weepy over being parted from him and here he was making plans for her to move to another country!

'That sounds great,' she said with false brightness. 'Can you give me Bryn's details and I'll email him when I get back? I could certainly use a bit of heat right now.'

'Um, I can give you the details, sure, but ... ' Liam finally turned to look at her. 'I guess I wasn't clear because, you see, the offer would be for both of us.'

'What do you mean?' she said quietly. 'Why would he offer you a job when you already have one here?'

'There's not much use for a ski instructor when there's no snow,' he said, smiling softly at her. 'Like you, I could do with a bit of heat but I'll be totally honest with you, I'd go anywhere — so long as it was with you.'

Rose blinked. Surely he hadn't just said that?

'Rose ... are you going to say something?' he asked, a crease appearing between his eyebrows.

'Yes!' she cried and launched herself at him, knocking him back onto the snow and landing on top of him.

'Yes to Spain, or yes to me being with you?' he asked, grinning up at her.

'Yes to both!'

'That is so what I wanted to hear! I've wanted to ask you for weeks now but I've been too nervous. I was worried you would say no.'

Rose laughed with joy as he spun her around so she was underneath him while he cushioned her head with his arm.

'Can I kiss you now?' he asked.

'Yes please,' said Rose, happiness bubbling through her veins.

Slowly he lowered his mouth and brushed her lips with his own. Her heart rate quickened and she pulled off a glove so she could touch the rough stubble of his jaw. He deepened the kiss, his mouth moving firmly over hers.

Part of the snowman broke off and landed on their heads, cold snow dripping onto their cheeks. Liam pulled away and they grinned at each other.

'Are you sure about Spain?' she asked. 'There won't be any mountains to plummet down.'

'The villas are near the sea. I can take up surfing.' He grinned, and then his expression became serious. 'I want to take a leaf out of your book and try something new. You're the bravest person I've ever met.'

'What if . . . ?' she began.

'Life is full of what-ifs,' he interrupted. 'I know that I want us to be together because I have fallen very much in love with you. Whatever life throws at us we can muddle through it together, as we have the last few months. I'll have to come back here next season, though. Do you think you'd be interested in joining me?'

She reached up and touched the silky ends of his hair.

'Luckily I've fallen in love with you too, so yes, I will come out here again next year.'

The crinkles around his eyes deepened as his warm smile broke across his face.

'I didn't bring any champagne with me, so shall we have another cup of hot chocolate to celebrate before we head home?'

'That sounds like a perfect end to the day,' murmured Rose, leaning against his arm.

As they gazed out at the majestic horizon Rose knew that it didn't matter where she travelled, because as long as she was with Liam she would always be home.

Other titles in the
Linford Romance Library:

WINGS OF A NIGHTINGALE

Alan C. Williams

It's 1941 when strong-willed Aussie nurse, Pauline Newton, arrives at Killymoor Hall, a British military hospital which has many secrets. Most crucially, it's a base for a team of Nazi saboteurs. Falling in love with the mysterious Sergeant Ray Tennyson, Pauline finds herself involved in murders, skulduggery and intrigue as they both race desperately to discover the German leaders' identity. Throughout it all, Ray and Pauline must resolve their own differences if they hope to stop the Nazis altering the War's outcome forever.

MURDER IN THE HAUNTED CASTLE

Ken Preston

Divorced Kim has come to terms with the fact that her only daughter is growing up. A last memorable holiday together before Maddie immerses herself in GCSE revision seems just the thing. But as if meeting the delectable James (no, not Bond — but close!) isn't exciting enough to throw a spanner in the works, just wait until they all get to the haunted castle. Dream holiday? More like a nightmare! But how will it end . . . ?

ISLAND OF MISTS

Evelyn Orange

Arasay — remote Scottish island, wildlife haven, and home to Jenna's ancestors. When she arrives to help out her great aunt in the bookshop, she's running from her past and hiding from the world. But she's not expecting to meet an attractive wildlife photographer who is also using the island to escape from previous traumas. As Jenna embraces island life and becomes closer to Jake and his family, there are secrets in the mist that could threaten their future happiness . . .

ONE MAN'S LOSS

Valerie Holmes

Sir Christian Leigh-Bolton had never intended to gamble that night the vultures circled around Sir Howard. Losing heavily and in desperation, Sir Howard foolishly wagers away his inheritance, Kingsley Hall — and Christian steps in and wins the prize. Sir Howard's actions leave his sister, Eleanor, virtually homeless. Christian's honour is further tested when he makes a promise to Sir Howard, a dying man, not knowing if he can fulfil it. Meanwhile, Eleanor has taken matters into her own hands …

JESSIE'S LITTLE BOOKSHOP BY THE SEA

Kirsty Ferry

Jessie Tempest has two main interests: reading books and selling books. Her little bookshop in the seaside town of Staithes is Jessie's sanctuary from the outside world. When writer Miles Fareham and his inquisitive eight-year-old, Elijah, arrive to stay in the holiday apartment above the shop, it's testing — Jessie has always felt clueless around kids. But soon she realises that first impressions aren't always the right ones — and, of course, you can never judge a book by its cover!